FOREVER HUNGER

DAVID M. SALKIN

ISBN-13: 978-0984923113
ISBN-10: 098492311X

This is a work of fiction. The characters, incidents and dialogues in this book are of the author's imagination and are not to be construed as real. Any resemblance to actual events or persons, living or dead, is completely coincidental.

FROM THE AUTHOR

As an author, your agent or publisher will tell you to "build your audience" and write stories in the same genre. This allows your readers to know what to expect when they see your name on the cover of a book. It makes sense, except for the fact that I like to write about a lot of different subjects—and aren't *I* allowed to have fun, *too*?

This book was *fun*. It has *evil* in it. It has violence and gore and blood. It even has s-e-x in it. (Which is horrifying for a dad to think his children may one day read scenes like that, written by their father, and may be scarred for life.) It also has heart ache and love and a bit of my sense of humor.

I've never understood why the public loves to read the same storyline over and over. These "formula" type vampire romances have become soap operas, in my humble opinion, and yet are wildly popular. While I do think vampires and other creatures that go bump in the night are great characters for stories, I'd like to think that the stories can be more than the "same ol' same ol'."

This story begins long ago but quickly takes you to New York City and becomes a rather twisted crime thriller. It doesn't fit into the typical vampire romance. It doesn't fit into the typical crime thriller. It isn't typical anything, really, from a publisher's standpoint. (They don't like that, either. They want a label for the genre!) We'll just call this an urban fantasy vampire romance crime thriller. That should cover it.

I hope you enjoy reading it as much as I enjoyed writing it.

DEDICATION PAGE

As always, for Patty and my family.

There's also a whole lot of other folks who I'd like to thank for any of the following—their friendship, their support, their inspiration, or the joy and fun they've brought into my life through their own talents. In no particular order...

The men and women who have served or are serving this great country all over the globe, especially the ones still recovering from their wounds. Led Zeppelin, The Doors, Hendrix, Boston, DMB, Hothouse Flowers, Rush, and brother Eric Salkin on sax. My friends in the Philip A. Reynolds Detachment of the Marine Corps League. The members of the Veteran's Community Alliance. Warren Zevon, one of the coolest song writers and performers ever. The Sunrise Optimist Club and Camp Quality, bringing smiles to children. Penguin Books, Tom Colgan and Doug Whiteman for that very first break with Crescent Fire. The person who invented banana cream pie. My IJO friends. The other authors out there who are banging away on their keyboards, refusing to give up! Stacey, Missy, Jesse, Jake, Mike, Syd Suspicious and family. Did I already thank the inventor of banana cream pie? How about Natalie... she bakes a mean one.

Thank you to April at Graphicfantastic for the beautiful cover and assistance in this project.

One

The Beginning

Sometimes, when Adam would "sleep", he would dream of the beginning—of life back in Prussia when his heart still beat with his *own* blood. His dreams always ended the same way though, with the nightmare that was the Battle of Jena, on October 14th, 1806.

Back in his human days, Adam Priest was still Olmer Bartha, a corporal in the Prussian Army that was fighting against Napoleon in what is today Germany. Olmer had fought in the army of Frederick Louis, a "General of Infantry" and the Prince of Hohenlohe-Ingelfingen. It was at the decisive Battle of Jena that Prince Hohenlohe led his force of 35,000 men against the Army of Napoleon, whose own troops numbered almost 100,000. Corporal Bartha, a lowly infantryman, had no way of knowing the forces they faced outnumbered them three to one, nor was he aware of the horrors that awaited him that day which would end his life, as he knew it, and begin the next.

By one in the afternoon of October 14th, the Prussian Army was shattered. While the French casualties numbered over 5,000, the Prussian Army death toll topped 25,000. As Corporal Bartha ran for his life with the remnants of his infantry regiment, the French Cavalry Commander Joachim-Napoléon Murat gave pursuit, slaughtering the fleeing Prussians by the thousands. The terrified young corporal had long ago dropped his musket and ran haphazardly with his panicked comrades as horses trampled through their defeated ranks, their merciless French riders swinging heavy sabers and lopping off heads and arms as they charged through the beaten infantrymen. Olmer took refuge in the woods, now buzzing with wounded and dying Prussians.

Olmer stumbled through the thick undergrowth, the long tails of his heavy green coat snagging vines and tree limbs as he fell and rose to run, over and over, crashing desperately through the thick forest. He was covered with cuts and scrapes from the branches and thorns. He ran until his lungs demanded that he walk, and then he walked for the remainder of the afternoon, until the pounding of cannons and long thunderous volleys of musketry faded away. As the sun disappeared from overhead, the air grew colder, and soon he could see his own breath. He was completely lost and without food—but he did have his canteen and was happy to still be alive.

The exhausted corporal sat against a huge tree and let his head fall back against the trunk of the ancient arbor. Pulling out his canteen, he gave it a little swish, remembering it was now only half full of water. He drank a few long sips and then carefully closed it. He took stock of what he had left on him: a heavy wool field blanket was still rolled and tied on his back. His long green coat was warm, with brown leather cartridge belts crisscrossed over his chest. His boots were knee high, under which he wore leggings and breeches which some weeks ago had been white. His knife was still in his belt, but that was his only weapon. He had lost his tall helmet, his musket and most of his ammunition, as well as his bayonet and his field pack. It had been a panicked retreat and was humiliating. With his head against the tree, completely exhausted, Olmer fell asleep.

Olmer awoke to the sounds of whispering in the dark. The woods, which under normal conditions would be devoid of human activity, were now home to small groups of terrified and wounded Prussians. Olmer heard his Prussian language being whispered and let out a slow sigh of relief. He carefully crawled on his hands and knees through the dark towards the sounds of footsteps and soldiers speaking in hushed voices. He moved cautiously, not daring to allow a branch to snap under him. When he was close enough to be sure it was the voices of other surviving Prussian soldiers, he called out quietly into the darkness.

"Hey! You! Out there! Corporal Bartha, second infantry regiment, B Company! Who is out there?"

The woods went quiet. He suddenly felt afraid, and knelt deeper into the underbrush. He could hear twigs snapping as people moved around ahead of him, and then on both sides of him. He dared not breathe, and didn't move a muscle.

"You there!" called out a hoarse whisper in Prussian. "Where are you?"

"In front of you. Who is there?" he whispered back. It was so dark he could barely see his own hand in front of his face.

A branch crunched behind him and he spun around to find two men upon him. The one in front moved forward towards him quickly and grabbed his coat, until their faces were close enough to see each other. They each quickly looked at the uniform of the other to make sure they were both truly Prussian soldiers.

"Corporal," acknowledged the man in front of him. Olmer looked at his arm. He wore the insignia of a sergeant. "You have water?"

Olmer pulled his shoulder strap over his head and handed it to the sergeant who took a long drink and handed it to the men behind Olmer. Olmer watched helplessly as the men behind him drank his canteen empty without ever asking him if it was okay or saving him a sip of the water he had carefully rationed.

"You have food?" asked the sergeant.

"No. Just the water. That was all of it."

The man behind him pulled at his blanket and demanded that Olmer give it to him. The sergeant ordered him to give it up, explaining they had a wounded man that needed it. Olmer had no choice but to unfasten his bedroll and have it ripped from his hands.

"It's cold. I need your coat," said one of the men behind him. That was too much.

"I can't give you my coat. I won't be out of uniform! I retreated into the woods, but I'm no deserter!" said Olmer forcefully.

The sergeant showed him a knife. "That was an *order* corporal. Give him your coat!"

Olmer was outraged, but was also outranked and outnumbered. He began to unbuckle the leather straps over his chest when something moved past them in the woods. He froze, as did his assailants.

"What was that?" whispered one of the men to the sergeant.

Whatever it was, it was moving quickly around them. Every time they thought they knew where it was, it moved again so quickly they found themselves spinning in circles.

"Wolf?" answered the sergeant, not knowing exactly what it was. He held his large knife out in front of him. His comrades pulled out their own bayonets and faced out from the center, trying to track the movements of whatever was circling them. Whatever it was, it was too fast to be human.

The sergeant pushed at his men. "Go on," he whispered, pushing them towards the noise in the darkness.

The two men moved slowly forward, weapons drawn in front of them. Whatever it was, it had stopped moving. As the men moved forward, the sergeant moved slowly in behind them, and Olmer slowly and quietly moved away backwards. He slipped away from them in the darkness and stayed low, now unable to see them. He did hear the sound of something move through the branches and the screaming that ensued.

Two

Olmer had backed away slowly in the darkness, feeling his way among the large tree trunks as he moved carefully over the large tree roots that caught his boots. He was at the fringe of knowing approximately where the trio of troublemakers were when the screaming began. The wolf, or *whatever* that was in the darkness, had attacked. He had heard the sound of the branches snapping and the thud of bodies colliding. The loud wail of one of the men was followed by shouting, and then screaming. Olmer's hair stood up on his arms as he heard the sounds of the three men being murdered. It was unlike anything he had ever heard.

In all the battles in which Olmer had participated, there had been horrible casualties. He had seen cannonballs remove limbs in front of him. He had seen men run through with bayonet and saber. He had seen hand to hand combat and the violence that goes with it. None of that was close to what he was hearing in the woods. Perhaps the darkness amplified his fear—perhaps it was not knowing exactly what was happening that was making it so much more terrifying, but the screaming of three men being torn to pieces was otherworldly. Olmer was sure Hell must sound exactly the same. The men who had taken his water and blanket were being torn to pieces by something that wasn't human, *that* was for certain. He could hear the men, who had moments ago been so rough and threatening, now begging for their lives and screaming in horrible agony. Whatever it was that was killing them remained silent. Olmer felt himself begin to cry in fear, something he had never done before even in the worst of battle. He wrapped his arms around his knees, seated against a tree, and rocked back and forth trying to calm himself so whatever was out there wouldn't hear him.

He was sure he heard a bone snap. It wasn't a branch—he had been hearing *that* all night. *This* was much louder and sharper, and there was a dull grunt after the noise. He sat, frozen in fear, and listened as something began to slurp and munch on the three Prussian soldiers in the dark. He prayed that *whatever* it was, it would be full before it decided to eat number four. As Olmer rocked back and forth in tears, gripping his knees tightly, he could hear the sounds of teeth scraping across bone, a skull perhaps.

· · ·

OLMER HAD ROCKED HIMSELF TO sleep eventually, his back still against that same mammoth tree. The sun breaking over the treetops sent rays of light filtering through the bare branches. As the forest came to life with the sound of birds, Olmer lifted his head off of his forearms and looked around. He was filthy, stiff, and very cold. He tried to remember where the attack had come from last night, playing back the event in his head as he scanned the forest. He listened for a long time before he dared move. There was no sound other than the birds. And he slowly stood and stretched his arms and legs. He traced his way back towards the location of the attack last night, moving quietly and slowly, lest that animal was still around. He came to the spot and froze.

Had the three men been standing together for a direct hit from a sixteen pounder, it might have explained what he was looking at. He stood, feeling numb, as he scanned the scene before him. What was left of the three men was torn to pieces and scattered all over the ground or strewn in the low tree branches. There were small pieces of flesh, hands, limbs, organs—they were *everywhere*. Olmer wretched, but had not eaten in almost two days, and nothing came up. He stood with his hands on his knees, dry heaving for a moment before starting to run away from the unbelievable carnage. He hadn't gone far when he came upon another Prussian soldier lying on the ground nearby.

Olmer stopped and looked down at the body. The soldier's uniform was filthy and covered in blood, but he was "whole" at least. The young man was lying in the fetal position, like he was serenely napping, and Olmer knelt beside him. Perhaps he had died peacefully? His tunic was slick with blood. Olmer reached for the man's neck to check for a pulse, but the man's eye's opened quickly and his hand shot out and grabbed Olmer by the wrist. Olmer jumped and let out a quick shout, but then smiled down at the man.

"My God! I thought you were dead!"

The young soldier smiled slowly, even his face had blood all over it.

"Yes, so did I," he said softly, a strange smile on his face.

"Were you here all night? Did you hear that attack?" asked Olmer, so relieved to find another living soul that he wanted to hug the stranger.

"I'm not sure. I fled to the woods when the French cavalry attacked. Most of my company was killed before making it here. After dark, I wandered for a bit and got lost, so I just stopped where I was and fell asleep. And you?" He sat up and faced Olmer, who was staring at the man's uniform.

Olmer was still looking at the man's tunic when he said quietly, "It was awful. I think the French butchers killed almost all of us. There were so many of them. Our lines broke. Their cavalry charged through us and never stopped. My friend…" he stopped speaking and his eyes welled up.

The man tried to stand, but settled back to the ground, wounded. "Yes," he said. "There was so much *blood*." He had a strange expression. Not a true smile—but certainly not Olmer's look of dread and shock.

"You are wounded?" asked Olmer, again looking at the blood soaked uniform.

The man raised his eyebrows and looked at his own torso, which was leaking blood into his clothing. "I think I am?" he said, in almost a question. "Impossible…" he said, his voice trailing off.

Olmer smiled. "Not so impossible. Be glad you are alive. Let me have a look," he said as he reached for the man's uniform.

The man again grabbed his wrist. "Impossible." He said again, this time his face showing anger.

Olmer slowly withdrew his hand and sat back, slightly unnerved. "You might be injured. You should let me have a look. We need to stop the bleeding."

The man looked at Olmer and began laughing—a long howling

laugh that turned into an earsplitting noise that sounded like the death throes of the men last night. Olmer's hair stood up and his eyes opened wide.

"I don't *bleed*! I don't *die*! I *am* dead!" howled the man, this time grabbing Olmer's wrists and pulling him closer. The man's face was glowing red as if with fever. His eyes looked wild, their blue color almost silver against the whites. "I *can't* die!" he said again, this time almost speaking to himself, but not letting go of Olmer, who winced in pain. The man's grip was so strong...

"You're hurting me," he grimaced. "You are with fever—relax and let me look at your wound..."

The man squeezed harder and bent one of Olmer's wrists, causing him to fall over on his side, and the man moved quickly on top of him, straddling his stomach with his strong legs. The wild-eyed Prussian looked around them. They were alone, except for the remnants of the three men in the trees.

He leaned closer to Olmer's face.

"You can't kill what is dead!" he hissed. He ripped open his blood soaked tunic and looked down at his own chest and abdomen. He had several very large holes in his body, made by many French musket balls. Mortal wounds to be sure—they appeared to go directly through his heart. They bled only slightly. "What is happening to me?" he asked himself, but out loud.

"You are wounded! Let me help you!" pleaded Olmer, not yet comprehending what he was actually seeing.

"I am *not* wounded!" hissed the man. "I am *dead*! I have been dead for *two hundred years*! But *never wounded*!" He sounded confused. He looked back down at his wounds, and pushed a finger deep into one of the holes. When he pulled it out, he sucked off the blood and stared at

Olmer with eyes that looked insane.

"This battle has ended me!" he hissed. He pushed two fingers back into the hole and pulled them out, this time they were dry. His color was changing from flushed fever-red to a whitening ashen color of death. "I can drink your blood and live another few hours maybe." He was now speaking to himself again. "Or I can give you my curse and live on forever through *you*!"

Olmer pushed himself back into the ground as hard as he could, trying to get away even though he was pinned against the forest floor. He was terrified of this mad man that held him with inhuman strength. "Please!" he pleaded, "*Please*! Let me *go*!"

"I will let you go when I am finished with you," he whispered, now leaning inches from Olmer's face. His breath was terrible, like something rotting, and his face was turning white as the whites of his eyes slowly yellowed. His once blue eyes were fading to pale silver.

Olmer was crying again. Surely he was seeing the devil himself. "*Please*!" he shrieked.

"I served with the Prussians—I served with the French—I served with the English...wherever there was war. Wherever the crusaders went. Wherever there was blood. I have been there—always on the fringe of death—watching, waiting for my chance to feed. I was *immortal*!" His breath was becoming ragged and wheezy now, and his rotten breath grew even more repulsive. He leaned closer, his teeth now pointed like some type of wild animal. Olmer opened his mouth to scream, but no noise would come out. His heart was pounding in his chest, and the creature on top of him placed his hand on Olmer's heart.

"I *feel* it!" he hissed. "I can *hear* it! Your blood pounds in your chest so hard I can *smell* it!" He leaned closer still, his razor sharp teeth now longer and extended out of his mouth. He inhaled deeply, smelling

Olmer's blood pounding in his chest. "I could feed on you right now—but it wouldn't help me. I know that now. I am dying. But *you*!" he hissed between ragged breaths, "You will live undead forever!" He bit deeply into Olmer's throat, his teeth tearing through Olmer's trachea. He exhaled deeply into Olmer's lungs, filling them with his breath of death as he expelled his own cursed blood into Olmer's throat. The Prussian soldier had disappeared—what was on top of Olmer now was pure evil—pure ungodly animal. Olmer was trying to scream as pain tore through his body. His head felt like it would explode, and his legs' kicked wildly under the beast that was coughing its curse of blood and evil air into Olmer's open throat.

Olmer kicked and struggled until he felt his world going dark. He couldn't breathe- couldn't get away—he was dying and he could feel panic giving way to surrender. He felt sadness at his own death…could feel his own life slipping away from him…helpless. The forest began to spin around him, and Olmer felt weaker as his life ebbed.

The creature pulled his face away from Olmer, panting like a wild beast, winded and wild. He spoke, but his voice was now a hoarse ragged wheeze. He had a crazed smile on his face, Olmer's blood running down his chin.

"You're one of *me* now!" it whispered. "Just as I was made in those dark cold mountains all those years ago, taken from the human world and cursed with never ending hunger, so shall *you* be cursed! You're not alive! You're not dead! *You are death itself!*"

Olmer lay there, feeling nauseous and paralyzed, looking up at this creature from the depths of Hell, and tried to pray to God. The words wouldn't come. His mind was confused, and his heart rate was slowing. He felt so sick. So cold.

The creature rolled off of him and began laughing wildly again, sounding like a broken musical instrument being played by Satan. He began screaming at the heavens, making no sense at all as his voice broke and went hoarse. He was speaking a language that was not Prussian as he rambled wildly. The creature opened his arms and shrieked, his skin now rotting before Olmer's glazed eyes. As the creature's flesh rotted, his eyes went dim and rotted back into their sockets, and his stomach collapsed upon itself as the final remnants of bodily fluid leaked into the forest floor.

Olmer rolled to his side, finally feeling like he could move, and proceeded to vomit up huge quantities of blood. He watched his blood coming up in huge surges, scared and horrified by what he saw. The creature before him was now turning to dust—gone from this world forever—but what had it done to him? He felt cold—so cold. He doubled over in agony and vomited for what seemed like hours as the last of his blood poured out into the grass and leaves, making them slick with thick red goo.

Olmer closed his eyes and died. His heart stopping, never to beat again with his own blood.

Three

Olmer awoke, his clothes drenched in his own blood. He was dazed, and felt sick. It was so quiet. He looked around, trying to remember what had happened. He remembered the battle. The slaughter of his comrades under the French cavalry. He remembered running into the woods. Nightfall. The attack. What *was* that? His hair stood up. The creature. He remembered now. That thing that he thought was a soldier—that thing he tried to *help*.

Olmer sat up and reached for his throat. It was sore, but not bleeding. He held his hand there, suddenly worried at how cold he felt. He felt for his pulse, but couldn't find it. He reached for his left wrist and tried there—nothing. He must be very weak, he told himself. He stood. The silence was such a contrast to the screaming and sounds of battle the days before. He cocked his head and listened. Listened so hard. He could hear noises he had never heard before. Sounds like breathing. Like hearts pumping. The slightest of sounds that must be so far away, and yet, he could *hear* them.

His stomach grumbled. He remembered now—vomiting so much blood. He opened his coat and looked at his own stomach and chest. He looked so white. Ashen. Sickly. But he didn't *feel* sick. What was wrong? He reached for his throat again and remembered that horrid thing that had bitten him. He shuddered as he remembered that thing breathing into his own lungs—that putrid smell. He dry heaved again, but nothing would come up. He realized he was hungry. He hadn't eaten since…when? The day before the battle. That was…three days now? No wonder he was so sick and weak.

Olmer decided to risk walking out of the forest. He needed to find food and water. He stopped and thought about that. He wasn't thirsty. He *should* be. When did he last drink? That night when the three soldiers stole his canteen. Strange.

Olmer walked for hours through the ancient forest, towards the battlefield. It was getting near dusk. Olmer should have been tired, but he wasn't. In fact, he was feeling better, not worse. When he reached the fringe of the forest, he stopped and looked out at the sight of the Jena battlefield. It was like looking at another planet. The landscape was scorched. The rolling plains were burnt and destroyed. Piles of dead and dying soldiers extended as far as he could see. Dead horses were everywhere, mixed with the men. Broken wagons, destroyed cannon caissons, even the large cannons themselves were littered about the landscape. The ground had been torn up and trampled by thousands of charging horses and fleeing men. Tattered flags and clothes fluttered in the light breeze under the dim autumn sun.

Olmer crouched down and looked. And listened. He could hear it again. That strange noise in his ears. Men crying. Breathing. Begging for water. For help. For God. He could hear beating hearts in a quiet chorus of pumping. So strange. He should have felt revulsion. Sadness. Horror. *Something.* Instead, he only felt hungry. Scanning in all directions for French troops and seeing none, he stepped out of the woods and walked towards the devastation. Twenty-five thousand dead countrymen and five thousand dead French, mixed with thousands of dead horses and mules...it had been a massacre. Olmer was starving.

He came upon a small group of dead Prussians. They were white and frozen in death, eyes still open but not seeing. One of them was now food for a large black bird that ignored Olmer as it pecked at an eye socket. Olmer ignored the bird, feeling nothing, and pulled off the man's canteen. He pulled out the cork and took a long swig. He spit it out and began vomiting although nothing would come up. He felt horribly ill. Perhaps the water had gone rancid? He smelled it. It smelled like a swamp. Disgusting. He tried another canteen. It was the same. Disgusting. And another, and another. All of the water was bad? He couldn't bring it to his lips without feeling sick.

His stomach tightened. He was starving. He rifled through the field packs and pockets of the dead looking for food until he found a piece of hardtack. He brought the old biscuit to his lips and the smell hit him. It smelled like weeds, or wood, or dirt...*whatever* it was, it wasn't *food.* He threw it on the ground and the birds went after it.

He walked, without purpose, through the battlefield. Whatever wounded who had been able to walk had already hobbled on to find help or the end of a French Bayonet. But then he heard someone calling for help. Olmer stopped and cocked his head. He closed his eyes and listened. Really *listened*. He walked towards the sound, amazed at how far away it was, but that he could still hear it. He found the source, a French soldier on his back clutching rosary beads and quietly awaiting death. The Frenchman had managed to tie off the leg wound that had almost severed his leg below the knee with a scarf. He opened his eyes and saw Olmer standing above him.

Olmer had never felt it before when looking at another human. Hunger. He felt a slight sense of nausea at what he was thinking, but it was too strong. He knelt beside the dying Frenchman and pulled the make-shift tourniquet off of his shredded leg. The blood immediately began to pump again from the wound near his knee where a cannonball had skipped by and shattered his lower leg bones. Olmer felt something in his mouth, and to his shock, realized it was his own teeth. He reached into his own mouth with his fingertips and felt razor sharp teeth extending out of his mouth as his body readied to feed. Olmer didn't feel panic or horror, only uncontrollable hunger.

The Frenchman looked at him and saw his mouth—saw his fangs, and whispered, "Mon Dieu!" Olmer knelt beside the man, closed his eyes and inhaled deeply. He could *smell* the blood. He could feel its warmth. He felt so *alive*! He let out a long howl like a beast from the forest, and surprised himself at his own noise, but he could feel an animal inside himself coming out. He couldn't stop it. Olmer pounced forward on the man's leg wound and used his fingertips, now armed with claws, to tear open the man's trouser leg and sink his teeth into the man's lower thigh. He bit hard and his fangs slid deep into the man's flesh. Warm delicious blood poured down Olmer's throat as he sucked as hard as he could. He ignored the man's screaming, listening instead to the sound of the man's heartbeat pounding louder and faster as the man panicked.

Olmer could taste the adrenaline pump into the man's bloodstream and felt it carry into his own body, his excitement now building at his first blood meal. "The animal was out" now, as Olmer would learn over time, and he was almost out of control. He bit through the man's leg deeper, in a feeding frenzy, and tore off a huge chunk of the man's thigh, which he chewed and swallowed in large chunks. The Frenchman was screaming at the top of his lungs and trying the beat the animal on his leg with his fists, but he was too weak, and could feel his life slowly draining from him with each loud slurp of the nightmare on top of him.

Olmer looked up at the man's face—saw the expression of complete and total terror, and let out a loud, long howl that filled the air for hundreds of yards. Large black birds took to the air at the sound, their fluttering wings adding to eerie sound of the dead landscape. He leaned forward and stared deeply into the man's eyes and smiled, blood and flesh running down his chin in a nasty drool. He pushed the man's head up, exposing his throat, and could actually hear the man's pulse in the carotid artery. He was crazed with blood lust and leaned in where he opened wide and ripped out the man's throat, sucking up the gushing flow of blood. He slurped and sucked deeply, swallowing mouthful after mouthful until his own body was warm and strong. For the first time that day, he could feel his own heart beating, although not with blood made his own body. As Olmer sucked the blood, he could feel the man die in his mouth, the blood becoming flat tasting, like old soda, as the lungs no longer pumped oxygen into the blood.

Olmer sat back and looked at the dead man in front of him. He should have felt horror and shame and disgust, but he didn't. Instead, he felt power. His hunger was gone. He felt stronger than ever, and totally calm. And then it happened. He leaned forward and vomited up the chunks of flesh he had eaten in a black bloody mess. He spit and cleared his mouth. Lesson learned. It was okay to drink the blood, but not to eat the flesh. He wished that thing that had created him was still alive to question. There was much to learn.

Four

New York City, 2011

Adam Priest woke from his dream and tried to remember where he was. When he was. He was in New York. It was 2011. Amazing. He looked around at the warehouse where he had fed last night and then had decided to stay and rest. He burped, tasting the woman from last night. Disgusting. The street walkers were always diseased and on drugs, but he had been hungry and this one was attractive to him at that moment. He loved the way he could seduce the prostitutes, who were usually so cold and "faking it" with their Johns. When he had them, he would surprise them with the use of his long tongue, making them scream in delight and send out a flood of hormones, adrenaline and pheromones, making their blood like a fine Cabernet, filled with subtle flavors. He had come a long way since his savage days in the forests of Germany.

This one had been particularly thrilling, although she has been a cocaine user which always made him feel sick the next day. He had allowed her to proposition him in a bar, then agreed to follow her to a cheap motel she knew about. When they neared a warehouse along the way to the hotel, he pulled her inside and told her how he loved it in public. When he dropped to his knees and pulled her skirt up to bury his face between her legs, she didn't resist. It wasn't until he sank his long fangs into her femoral artery that she protested anything he had done to her. She had started to scream, but Adam had reached up with his left hand and squeezed her throat so hard she couldn't make a sound. He sucked her blood slowly, enjoying the many flavors of her blood chemistry. She had obviously been seriously turned on by him before he bit into her, and she was one of his better meals in a long time. When he was full, and she was empty, he laid back and savored the taste, quite cheerfully. He could feel every nerve ending in his body—nothing short of complete euphoria. He allowed himself to sleep for a few hours, something he rarely did until he had gotten rid of the body, but she had been so delicious, he didn't want to ruin the moment.

Adam dreamt of his creation, the fateful night in the woods after the Battle of Jenna, back when he was human. He awoke confused for a moment, almost drunk on the many chemicals in that whore's blood, but smiled as he recalled his evening. He got up, picked up the dead woman like she weighed nothing, and threw her over his shoulder. The warehouse was huge and abandoned, and one he had used before. He walked into a rear storage area where an old furnace still sat, and pushed her body into it. He grabbed the gasoline can he had used before as well and doused her thoroughly before lighting her up. With very little fluid left in her body, she burned easily as Adam shoved pieces of gas soaked wooden pallets in with her. Watching her flesh roasting, he felt sad. It smelled good, under the gasoline vapors, and he missed being able to eat. She would have been tasty, he was sure. Oh well. His belly was quite full and his body was warm and strong. He inhaled her one last time, and then hustled out back into the street to head home.

Five

NYPD – Midtown North Precinct

"Captain, I'm sorry to bother you with this, but I've got another missing hooker, and 'her girls' are making a huge scene downstairs," said Sergeant Ruiz to Captain Ammiano, who had just hung up his phone.

"So send it over to missing persons," he grumbled.

"I told them that, and they say they *did* four days ago. They say she's dead. No way she'd just disappear for this long."

"Any evidence of a homicide?" asked the captain.

"No 'evidence' of *anything*, Cap. Just a disappeared hooker. But she's number four this month. The LT said to bring it to you. Wants to know if we should open a possible homicide file. Maybe these are connected. What do you want me to do?" asked Sergeant Ruiz.

The captain leaned back in his ancient green "leatherette" chair, which let out a long rusty squeak. He put his hands on top of his bald head and locked his fingers together there. "Number four, huh?"

"Yeah. But you know—we get two or three a month every month. They usually turn up OD'ed in the Hudson or under some culvert in the park. LT has a bug up his ass, though. Says we should be looking at these."

"He gonna' work the case with me?" asked Captain Ammiano.

"Says he will."

"Okay, send him up," he grumbled.

"What about the chicks downstairs? They got the whole Sisterhood Union down there. They say they ain't leaving until they talk to the Chief!"

Captain Ammiano laughed. "The *Chief*, huh?" He let the chair bring him back up to vertical and stood up. "Guess they'll have to settle."

Ammiano and Ruiz walked down the stairs together, the stairwell filled with smoking cops who couldn't smoke 'inside the building'. They traveled down through the blue haze into the first floor hallway, which was buzzing with activity. Midtown Manhattan was a busy place, and the Precinct was always hopping. Sgt. Ruiz led his captain to a group of five women in rather interesting attire ranging from a black leather miniskirt that showed thigh highs with a white corset top, to a very torn pair of pink sweats that said "Juicy" on the back, in between holes that showed a red thong, with matching braless tank top.

As soon as they spotted Sgt Ruiz again with a man in an officer's uniform, they descended on him like sharks to chopped tuna. "Juicy" was obviously the spokeswoman for the group.

"You the Chief?" she barked as they approached.

"I am Captain Patrick Ammiano, head of this precinct. I understand one of your 'associates' went missing four days ago?"

"That's right! And I went to missing persons and did a hundred pages of *bullshit* and nobody did anything since. They didn't even *look* for Tiffany!" The others began chiming in, all at once.

"Okay, listen," said the Captain, raising his hands to quiet the women, "Let's relax and get some statements and see if we can find your friend, okay?"

That led to everyone talking at once again, and Sergeant Ruiz shouted a "Shut up!", then followed it with a, "Please!" He had the group follow him down another hallway and sit on a bench, then, one at a time, give statements to himself and Captain Ammiano. When the last one was finished, she gave her cell number to the captain who gave her his card, and told her he'd contact her in a few days and to contact him if they heard anything or thought of anything that might be useful.

When they left, Captain Ammiano called Lt. Alexander into the room with him and Ruiz.

"Okay, best I can tell, a hooker named Tiffany, whose real name nobody seems to know, left Donavan's Pub off Columbus Circle around two in the morning with a white guy that no one can describe. Medium build, medium height, medium eyes, medium hair...nobody noticed anything. The one chick that was with Tiffany, named..." he checked his notes, "named Star, she says the guy looked clean cut, and was maybe 35 or 40, and in good shape. That's it."

"Bartender remember anything?" asked the lieutenant.

"Nothing. Place was crowded. Usually remembers people by what they drink—this guy comes up blank."

"Great. So we have a hooker with no real name. A suspect with no real description. Any other solid leads?" asked the LT.

"Nope," replied the captain. "But since you wanted to open a case file on her—she's all yours. Sergeant Ruiz will be more than happy to help you out with her. Personally, I am fishing for two weeks—you guys have fun." With that, Captain Ammiano got up and left, leaving Sgt. Ruiz and Lieutenant Alexander sitting at the bare metal table with a few papers for their newly opened case file.

"What are we supposed to do with this?" asked Roy. "We have nothing to work with. Nobody else to talk to. This is a dead end, LT."

"She might be, but she might also be connected to the other four missing hookers I have shoved in a file in my office. These girls have all gone missing without a trace. If they were somebody important, we'd be all over it—but nobody gives a shit because they're hookin'. We could have a serial killer out there, Roy, but any time I use that word, people look at me like I have three heads. I am not being hysterical or paranoid or any of the other bullshit comments I have heard about this—I am being professional. We've got somebody out there whacking young girls and it's about time we started acting like investigators."

Roy made a scowl, then leaned back and said, "Okay, boss. You're right. We should look at them as a possible series of attacks that have some connection. You have files on all the other ones?"

"I have very incomplete files on them. Same problems as with this case—no real names for most of them. No real backgrounds, no witnesses, no nothing. And I've only got the missing girls in *our* precinct. Now that Pat has given me a green light, I am going to contact the other precincts and start using some computer time to see what else I come up with."

"Can't we just use the supercomputer and have all the pictures of everyone with last known addresses up in like thirty seconds?" asked Roy.

"What are you talking about?" asked the lieutenant.

"You know—like the one on CSI. They get all the information they need in under a minute. Why don't we have one of those?"

Joe sat back, realizing that Roy was messing with him. "Very nice, Roy. Just for that, *you* can do the backgrounds. Shouldn't take you more than a minute…"

Lieutenant Alexander got up and left, throwing his file at Roy, who shook his head and mumbled, like there was any doubt who was actually gonna' do all of the work…

Six

Adam's Apartment

Adam returned to his apartment while it was still dark outside and closed the door behind him. He walked across the fairly empty loft towards his bed, undressing as he walked. He hung his clothes back up in the closet and laid down, nude, on his bed. He still felt very warm from his large blood meal, and was quite content. He lay on his back, and stared at the ceiling, thinking about his very long afterlife.

He had learned quickly, although somewhat reluctantly, what was required to survive. The few words that the creature had spoken had been a small clue. It had lived "on the fringe of the battlefields", finding blood meals easily, and disappearing without raising suspicion. With thousands of dead bodies, who would ever question a few more?

For several years after becoming what he was now, he had stayed in uniform. He changed sides whenever the thought suited him, becoming bored with one place or another after a while. No longer having friends or family he dared be around, lest he get hungry, he had no ties to any one place in particular. His parents and younger brothers would have been told about his presumed death at Jena, along with twenty-five thousand of his countrymen, and he was free to simply "disappear".

He had learned to control his appetite, feeding once every three days. On occasion, "the animal would get out", and he would go on a small rampage, sometimes drinking several victims at once. During these times, he would sometimes eat the flesh of some of his victims, making himself quite sick in the process. The blood meals were all that he needed to survive, and in fact, more than that would lead to vomiting up anything that was solid. Still, he missed "eating", and when he was lost in his animal frenzy, he would get carried away and end up making himself sick the way a drinker might go on a binge.

Now, two hundred years later, he was much more in control, and in fact, had become quite the connoisseur of blood. In his earlier years, he would eat any living mammal he could get his hands on. And while any mammal could sustain him and keep him alive, they equated to drinking wine from a box, and he had developed quite expensive taste over the years.

With his heightened senses, he had learned to "experience" blood the way a wine connoisseur appreciates the finest wines. His favorite, no doubt, was the blood of women who were experiencing sexual ecstasy, since they would release hormones, pheromones, endorphins, and even adrenaline. They also reminded him of being human, and provided female company, even if it didn't last long. While most of his human "feelings" had left him along with his soul, he did still feel lonely on occasion. Being physically with a woman was nostalgic, and he thoroughly enjoyed smelling and tasting the subtle differences in his prey.

Sometimes, when he had gone four or five days without eating, for various inconvenient reasons, he would pick a larger male—preferably one in good physical shape. The large, muscular males had less body fat, a taste he loathed, and they provided extra adrenaline when they fought back. Adam had somehow become much stronger after he had "died", and no human was a match for him—especially once his razor sharp claws and teeth had come out. More than one "tough guy" had frozen in fear when Adam's teeth grew out of his mouth. He could smell fear as easily as he could smell blood, and he enjoyed every second of it. He frequently tortured or killed his victims slowly, not out of malice or sadism, but rather because of the huge array of chemicals humans released when they were in agony, or fighting for their lives. The taste of a hyperventilating human with over-oxygenated blood—ahhh, it was like the finest champagne.

Adam's mind wandered, and he recalled a runner he had eaten in central park some years ago. The man had been an athlete, and his blood was so heavily oxygenated that he could practically taste the "fizz" on his tongue when he drank the man's blood. That meal had been so delicious he had gone slowly, keeping the poor man alive for almost an hour. He had snapped various bones in the man's hands to keep the adrenaline and endorphins pumping, watching the man's tormented face with great interest as he occasionally sipped the fine blood from his carotid artery. He had almost felt pity for a fleeting moment—a brief flirtation with some humanity left within him, but it was quickly suppressed with a long slurp of blood. In the end, he had left the man's body completely drained, and was so full, he didn't feed again for four days. The man's body was never found, having been shoved into an ancient sewer pipe. Adam's rapture lasted for days.

Adam looked at the ceiling, lost in his thoughts, traveling over the years and visiting the many places in his mind. Sometimes, after a large meal, he would "sleep" like this for two days or more, enjoying the scenery in his head. Adam, while he was still Olmer Bartha, had traveled west through Europe, following the armies, until he reached Western France. It was while there, several years after the Napoleonic Wars had ended, that he had learned about Prussian mercenaries traveling to America to fight in the Union Army in the "War Between the States". He was intrigued. The war would provide him with a food source, and he would have a chance to discover a new world. Why not?

Olmer joined a group of Prussians, boarded a large boat, and sailed west. Of course, by the time the boat arrived in New York City, most of the Prussian mercenaries had "disappeared", and Olmer had to sneak off of the ship to avoid questions at the port. He joined a New York regiment, and spent the next three years gorging himself across the American countryside. Places like Gettysburg, Fredericksburg and Antietam had provided so much food, he would occasionally leave his unit to feed for weeks, and then rejoin a unit somewhere else. After Appomattox, he returned to New York, and enjoyed life in the big city. Meals were plentiful, as were sights of interest and places to live without raising suspicion.

By the 1940's Olmer had changed his name to Adam Priest. He found this private joke to be most entertaining, naming himself after "the first human", and picking a last name to mock a church that spoke of God and Heaven and Hell. How would they explain *him*? Certainly, Satan had not spoken to him directly, and he had done nothing to bring this situation upon himself. So why him? Where was God? In over two hundred years of contemplation, he was no closer to any answer.

The new "Adam Priest" enlisted in the Army in 1942, went to Africa and then Europe, and ate his way to Berlin. He stayed there for a few years after the war, happy to hear a version of his old native tongue which came right back to him, but soon wanted to be back in America. He returned to America, and toured across the country for almost thirty years before returning to New York. No other city had the exciting night life, which made feeding so much easier. The huge population and wide variety of ethnicities offered a veritable "buffet"—it was like eating in a new country every night!

Adam decided New York City would be home for a long while, and money was never a problem, having steadily built his personal wealth from the wallets of his food. Adam found hunting easier at night, since he could see quite easily in the dark and his pray could not. While "vampire legends" claimed sunlight would burn him, it did not. He was as comfortable in the daylight as he was in the evening. The only thing he had to be careful about was being outside during the day when he hadn't eaten for a few days. When he was getting hungry, his skin would get quite pale and his eyes would get very light and silvery. While it didn't physically "bother" him, it did make his appearance quite bizarre, and he preferred to avoid attracting attention to himself.

When Adam was "full", his eyes were blue, as they had been in life. How many times had some woman leaned in close, flirting with unknown death, to whisper, "You have the most beautiful eyes" to him? They had seen those same eyes go wild as their own lives were sucked from their bodies.

Prior to 9-11, Adam found it quite easy to change his apartment every year or two as he moved around the city. He never stayed anyplace too long, afraid to be noticed by neighbors. After 9-11, renters began requiring identification and personal information that Adam was uncomfortable supplying. Because of this, he found an apartment in a nice part of the city, in midtown near Central Park, settled in, and stayed put.

Seven

Mid-Town Precinct

Sgt. Ruiz was sitting in his tiny office, on hold again. He had been on the phone on and off for three days trying to work the investigation into the missing Prostitute known only as "Tiffany". Fingerprints would have identified her easily, since she had been arrested for solicitation once before, but they were still waiting for Tiffany's "girls" to come back and go through log books of women that had been arrested for prostitution. They had left a message for "Star" to come back in, but she hadn't showed up yet. Obviously, she had a very busy schedule.

The voice finally came back on the phone again. "Hey, sorry, Roy—you still there?" asked a female voice.

"Yeah, but I think I need to shave again," he said sarcastically.

"Yeah, well, I think I may have something for you. I am transferring you to Detective Tim Rosetto's line. If he doesn't answer, you'll go to his voice mail. One of my guys down here told me that Tim is working a similar case. Good luck. Please hold." She put him back on hold, and transferred Roy to Tim's line. He expected a voice mail message, but Detective Rosetto picked up right away.

"Detective Rosetto here," he said quickly. He sounded like he was being interrupted.

"Detective Rosetto, this is Sergeant Roy Ruiz, Midtown. I'm working on a possible homicide. We have a Jane Doe, goes by Tiffany, officially listed as 'missing', but she was a working girl, and her friends are convinced she got waxed. I understand you are working some missing hookers?"

"Hey, Roy. Yeah, me and my partner have been working a couple of missing persons, and in the process have come up with a huge fucking pile of missing hookers. I know we lose a few in this city every month, but I think it's a lot more than we *think* it is."

"How many files you have open?" asked Roy.

"Okay, listen—this is under wraps, okay? I mentioned serial killer to my boss and he went ape-shit on me, capiche?"

Roy smiled. "Yeah, same reaction over here. Everyone is afraid of the New York Post headline. Whatcha' got?"

"Unofficially, Roy…almost forty. And I am pretty sure I am only scratching the surface."

"*Forty?*" Roy's jaw dropped. "How many years you go back?"

"Not years. *Months.* Fifteen months. It's not once a month, it's like a once every week or two. They're from all over the city. I am doing exactly the same thing you are doing—calling around to other precincts to see who is doing what. You are the first guy other than me to follow up."

"You have time for a cup of joe? I'll even buy."

"Not today—I'm jammed. You working tomorrow?"

"Yeah. Want me to come down there, or you want to come uptown?"

"You're buying! I'm coming uptown. I love the Starbucks by the Mandarin. Be there at eight?"

"You got it. I'll be in uniform."

"Done. I'm plain clothes. Look for an extremely handsome Italian stallion." He hung up.

. . .

ROY WAS BURIED IN PAPERS dating back almost two years when his phone rang. It was Lieutenant Alexander.

"Hey Roy—it's Joe. Come downstairs. You're gonna do some real cop work today."

"I *am* doing real cop work. I'm up to my ass in this missing persons shit that's not a serial killer, but makes people disappear every few days…got a lead from a detective in the sixth."

"Sixth? Isn't that the Village?"

"Yeah."

"Okay—good. In the meantime, we have an actual body. Sort of."

"Sort of?"

"Yeah. You didn't eat yet did you?"

"No. Why?" he asked warily.

"'Cause I don't want you puking on my good shoes. Come on down. I'm double parked in front."

"Double parked in front of a precinct? You got balls. I bet you get a ticket." He hung up, closed the files, and headed downstairs.

Eight

Crime Scene: Warehouse on 61ˢᵗ

oy had hopped into the car with Joe and they sped through the streets with their magnetic light stuck to the roof of their unmarked car.

"You were there already?" asked Roy.

"Yeah."

"And I take it, it's nasty?"

"Yeah."

"So why are you making *me* look at it? You pissed off at me or something"

"Yeah."

"What the fuck did I do?" asked Roy.

"You made the captain open up this missing persons file."

"You *told* me to!"

"Yeah."

Roy leaned back against the headrest and shook his head. "Great."

Joe began to speak, this time being serious and choosing his words carefully. "Remember how we talked about a serial killer, and when we mentioned it to the captain, he got pissed?"

"Yeah. Same shit happened over at the sixth."

"Yeah, well—I think we may have to rethink that."

"Oh shit, man. Am I going to be walking into some kind of bloody mess?"

"Nope. No blood. Not much of a mess really at all. But somebody did something really ugly and covered his tracks. I've got forensics over there taking pictures now."

They drove a few minutes in silence when Roy said, "My third grader got a note sent home from school the other day."

"Yeah? What did he do?"

"Taking a test on New York. Teacher asked him how many people lived in New York City, and my kid says, 'too fucking many, and they're driving in front of me'. He was quoting his father, evidently."

His lieutenant roared. They pulled over in front of a building where two squad cars and two unmarkeds sat out front. A patrolman was standing at the doorway taking notes from a very upset looking older man. Joe pointed to the older civilian.

"So that guy goes into the warehouse. He's a realtor. Trying to sell this old warehouse to a guy that wants to convert it to high-end residential units. He says he smelled something burning, and he walks around until he finds an old furnace. It's an ancient commercial boiler setup hooked up to the garbage shoot. He opens the door and makes a little discovery."

"Oh shit."

"Yeah."

They got out of the car and walked into the building where a medical examiner and a field technician were taking pictures, dusting for prints, and looking for evidence. Roy followed Joe to the furnace and Joe pointed with his thumb. Joe leaned in closer and got a whiff of burnt wood mixed with burnt human. He looked inside and saw three human skulls. One of them was broken up pretty badly, but two were still easily identifiable as human.

"Oh Jesus," he said quietly.

"He's not a suspect," said Joe.

"Who?" asked Roy, visibly shaken by what he was looking at.

"Jesus. We ruled him out. He was more of a 'love your brother' kind of guy. Not a 'kill your brother and burn him up' sort of dude. You okay?"

"Yeah. Shit."

The lieutenant pulled a zip-lock baggie out of his pocket. There was a sterling silver bracelet in it with a heart charm attached to it.

"Whatcha' got?"

"This is a Tiffany bracelet. Silver bracelet with a heart charm that is engraved with 'Tiffany' on it. Star had given me a description of this piece when I interviewed her. Said she gave it to Tiffany as a present last year. I'll show it to her. Probably a million of these things floating around the city, but its something, anyway."

"You pull that out of the fireplace?"

"No. If it had been in there, doc says it would have melted. Most of the bones are charred pretty good. It was a hot fire. The guys found it over by some pallets. They are still looking for hair and fibers."

"You think he killed three people at the same time and burned the bodies, or you think it's a dumping ground?" asked Roy.

"Not one hundred percent sure, but we think a dumping ground. I spoke to the M.E. and he says that the skulls were burned to different degrees. One of them had been there for longer than the other two, we're guessing. The other two are pretty similar in fire damage."

"But it isn't a serial killer," said Roy softly to no one in particular.

"Not until the chief says so. But I tell you what—this is some fucked up shit."

Nine

Columbus Circle

Roy was standing in his uniform drinking a "vente"—fancy name for an entire pot of coffee poured into a cup for one person. He had another sitting on the small counter for his blind date. He didn't pay much attention when the extremely obese man entered the Starbucks. The fat man walked directly towards him. Roy was thinking it was a tourist spotting him in uniform and about to ask for directions or something when the man extended a huge right hand and asked, "Ruiz?"

Roy looked at him and smiled. "I take it you are the Italian Stallion?"

"Well, you're half right, and we'll just leave it at that. That mine?" he asked, pointing to the huge coffee.

"Yeah. I guess I should have gotten some doughnuts too, huh?"

"Hey! No fat jokes. It's a medical condition."

"Yeah? Sorry."

Rosetto laughed. "Yeah, I have a pasta allergy. It makes me blow up like a fucking blimp, but I can't stop eating it." He laughed at his own bad joke and Roy just started at him, amazed at his size.

"I got a break in the case I'm working on. Let's take these and walk," he said, not wanting to talk in front of anyone. He looked at the big man and wondered if he could walk. It was like Tim read his mind.

"I know what you're thinking—when I haul ass I have to make two trips—but don't let the size fool ya'. I can still move when I have to."

Roy said nothing and walked out into the street with Mr. Good Year behind him. They walked, carrying their gallon cups of coffee (into which Tim had poured four sugars and a bottle of light cream).

"Yesterday I got called out to a warehouse. Forensics is still finishing their report, but we have at least three DB's in there. Well, sort of."

"How do you *sort of* have three dead bodies?" asked Tim, sipping his coffee.

"They had been packed into a furnace and burned."

"*Managia*," he cursed in Italian. "I hope they were dead first."

Roy's hair stood up. It had never occurred to him that they might have been *alive*. "Yeah," he said softly. "Anyway, we think one of the bodies may be a Jane Doe we are looking for. The last one that just came in. This hooker named Tiffany. She had a Tiffany bracelet when last seen, and one that matches the description was found at the scene."

"What about the other two?"

"Nothing. And dental records probably won't help. They were in bad shape. The rest of the scene looks pretty clean. We have a few partial prints off the door of the furnace, but they might not even be the killer's."

"Well, at least you have something. You started looking at this stuff when?"

"Just a couple of days ago."

"Yeah, well, you're a lucky son of a bitch. I've been busting my ass on this missing hooker file for *months* and I got '*gotz*'—*nuthing*!"

"Yeah, well, I'd rather be lucky than good. May not even be our missing Jane, but I am thinking it probably is. I stopped by the lab late yesterday. The doc I spoke to gave me some unofficial skinny, but it's fucked up, man."

"Yeah, well, 'fucked up' started when he put three bodies into a furnace and burned them," said Tim.

"The doc said our killer must have had a dog or something with him. Like…" he paused and looked around, feeling disgusting even speaking the words, "Like, he may have fed the parts to his dog before he burned them."

Tim lowered his coffee and made a sick face. "He *what*?"

"There were some large teeth marks on some of the bones, but they weren't human teeth. More like large fang marks or something. Like a real big dog or wolf or something. The doc was comparing the bite marks against a pretty big library of teeth impressions, and he said it was bigger than an average sized dog. Maybe the killer has a pet wolf or tiger or some shit. Doc never saw anything like it before. And this is coming from a guy that's been in the Big Apple for twenty years—he has seen some *shit*, know what I'm sayin'?"

"Yeah—whatever they pay the guys down the basement ain't enough. Bad enough we have to find some of the shit *we* see—but *those* guys have to *touch* it and take it apart. Who *wants* that job, anyway?"

"I hear ya'. Just seeing the furnace was enough to keep me up last night. I kept wondering what he had done to the three people before he burned them up. When I heard that shit about the teeth marks, it got to me, man."

They had crossed the street at Columbus Circle and sat down on a bench at the south end of Central Park. Tim took up half the bench.

"How many years you on?" asked Tim, watching a horse and buggy full of tourists trot by.

"Thirteen. You?"

"Almost twenty. Been a homicide detective for eleven. Let me tell ya', Roy—I have seen some fucked up shit in this city. I had a serial rapist-slash-killer about five years ago. He was a sick sonofabitch. He sexually assaulted and raped seven women before strangling them to death. I had the privilege of catching him in the act on a stakeout. It was only the second time I had ever fired my weapon. I just about blew that piece of shit's head off. Really shook me up when it happened. The girl was totally freaked. She was naked, beaten up pretty good. It wasn't until DNA came back that confirmed he was the same guy in the other attacks that I could sleep again."

Roy listened, sipping coffee, not really sure why Tim was telling him all this.

"Anyway, after that, I never thought I'd be able to draw my weapon again, ya' know? Even though that prick deserved what he got, I had actually killed somebody, and it was hard to shake off. I put on a hundred pounds after it happened. I guess you call it food therapy."

"At least you ain't an alcoholic like most of the guys I know," said Roy, trying to make light.

"Yeah—I guess that was the choice—eat or drink my way through it. Somehow hot fudge sundaes were better than booze. I would have fucked my way through it, but my wife split after it happened. Said '*I changed*'. Apparently I wasn't that much fun to be around."

Roy grunted. Most of his cop friends were divorced or on marriage number two or three. He fit in category one.

"Anyway, my point is this," said Tim, leaning closer to Roy. "I didn't think I'd ever be able to pull my gun again. *Ever*. But if I ever catch a guy who kills dozens of women, feeds them to his dog, and burns them after—I'll blow his fucking head off."

"Amen, brother," said Roy quietly.

Ten

Adam

Adam opened his eyes and looked around his studio apartment. It was Sunday afternoon, and he could hear the soft chiming of bells. Adam walked to his window and looked out on the city. It was quiet in terms of street traffic, but the weather was nice and there were lots of pedestrians about. He looked out towards Central Park and decided early evening would be a nice time to go outside and "people watch".

Like many humans, Adam was often entertained by watching people go by on the street. He had a few cafes where he would order espresso and sit outside. While he never drank his coffee, he would sit for an hour or more and wonder about the people that hustled by. New Yorkers were an exciting breed. They walked faster than any other humans on the planet, always in a hurry, always avoiding eye contact lest someone say "hello" and pose a huge threat. He found it curious, but interesting. Sometimes he would inhale the scent of various passersby, and know which ones were sick, which ones had had sex recently and not showered, which ones used expensive perfume. It was a game he played to pass the time, and time had become an interesting concept.

Many days were spent wondering about time. Day and night made no difference to him, and he had no internal clock that signaled sleep when it was dark outside. But it wasn't the days and nights he wondered about—it was the decades and centuries. How old was the creature that bit him in Jena? Why did it die? Did he also have a lifespan like humans, and if so, how long? Why did the creature that killed him die—was it the many wounds it had suffered during the battle?

In all of the time Adam had spent in the world, he still had not answered the majority of his own questions. He had on occasion read up on vampires, the hereafter, supernatural powers—the topics were endless, especially since the advent of the internet and access to infinite information. He found almost all of it to be fictional bullshit. While he was intrigued at the idea of Dracula and other vampire stories he read, he laughed at so much of it. He couldn't turn into a bat no matter how hard he tried. He didn't sleep in dirt or in a coffin and found the idea ludicrous. Warm soft sheets, preferably warmed by a female body before a meal would be his ideal place to sleep—not in some death box.

That last thought, while sitting at a café later that afternoon, blended into a woman walking by in a beautiful fur coat. It wasn't particularly cold, but in New York City, nothing was ever out of place. He remembered sleeping on a bear rug once a hundred years earlier while in France, and had a nostalgic moment. He decided he wanted a fur coat—either to wear or to sleep on, he hadn't decided yet, but he *would* have a fur coat.

He left a few dollars for the waiter and got up, walking quickly until he caught up with the pretty woman in her long gray fur. Adam never felt cold, really. Simply put, he was always cold. And quite dead. It wasn't until he fed and pints of hot blood rushed into his body that he felt "different", which was to say, "warm". At those moments, with a body full of blood pumping through his own heart, he felt alive again and something that could be almost called "happy". He wanted to be happy again.

He walked for quite a while, following the woman uptown towards the Museum of Natural History. When she got close to the museum, she turned right into Central Park, and Adam smiled to himself. In his mind, he made a wager with himself that she was heading across the park to the Metropolitan Museum of Art. She had that New York City walk, confident, and her hair probably cost her a few hundred dollars at some salon uptown. As he got closer, he could smell perfume that was no doubt very expensive. He still hadn't seen her face, and was getting curious. The coat was, however, beautiful. He was sure it would feel very soft under his naked dead body.

He walked slower and allowed her to get ahead, avoiding any suspicion. When she walked out of the park and headed towards the huge steps of the MET, he smiled wickedly. Of course—where else would this snotty little bitch be going?

He walked faster and followed her in. She was checking her coat, which was unexpected and for some reason made him very angry. He didn't want other hands on it. (It was already his, as far as he was concerned.) He managed to keep the animal inside—under control, and quietly followed the woman into the gallery. She got in line to pay for admission with Adam behind her. She felt him behind her and turned around, catching him off guard with a beautiful smile framed with deep red lipstick. Her teeth were white and perfect, and her own green eyes twinkled. If he had a heart that beat, it might have skipped one.

"Are you here for the Gellman exhibit?" she said with a sweet voice that was not bitchy at all—in fact, it was clear and crisp and sweet to his sensitive ears.

"Of course," he said, his own silvery eyes shining with a hunger she could not guess.

"I was *so* excited when I heard they'd have an exhibit here this week," she said.

In over a hundred years in New York, this was the first friendly face of innocence he had seen that actually caused him to feel sadness at not being human. He was staring at her, taking her in, smelling her, listening to her blood rush back and forth in her arteries when a nasty woman behind the counter shouted, "Next!"

She turned to pay for her ticket, but Adam quickly rushed up next to her and said, "Two, please."

She looked up at him and gave him another huge smile. "Don't do that!" she said. "I'll pay for my ticket—"

"Please," he said softly, in his most disarming voice, "It would be my great pleasure." He handed the woman a crisp hundred dollar bill, one of several he had taken off of the last dead whore he had eaten, and took the two tickets. "Would you do me the honor of walking through the exhibit with me? If you are an expert of Gellman, I'd love to learn more about him."

"Really," she said sarcastically. Her innocent face went sour.

"What? Have I offended you?" he asked.

"No. But I am pretty sure you offended Lisa Gellman."

If he had any blood inside his body, he might have blushed. "Ah. Mr. Gellman is a *Mrs*. So you see how little I know of her work."

"Um *hmm*," she said, with a suspicious smile.

"Will you walk the show with me for a bit?" he asked again, surprising himself that he actually cared. A moment ago, all he wanted was her soft coat that smelled like expensive perfume, and perhaps all of her bodily fluids. Now he actually wanted her company. Strange.

"For a bit," she said warily. The New Yorker in her was creeping out. They were a jaded bunch, and she had already been friendlier than any he had met that weren't drunk at a bar.

They walked in silence towards the hallway leading to the exhibit until she finally blurted, "So—what's your name?"

He stopped and smiled. He hadn't given his name to anyone in so long he almost said Olmer, but extended his hand and said, "Adam. Adam Priest. So very pleased to make your acquaintance."

She shook his hand, with a womanly grip that was firm enough to show confidence but still feminine. "Sara Lockhart. Nice to meet you, Adam." She smiled, a little flirt in it, and began walking again.

They entered the gallery where Lisa Gellman's work was being displayed, and Adam was surprised to see they were photographs, not paintings. Most of her portraits were done in black and white, although she had some very large color shots hanging as well. They walked together without speaking until they approached her first series of pictures, hung together of the same nude model. It was a young woman in black and white, and none of the shots showed her face. The photographer had seemed most interested the figure's lower back and buttocks, which were shown arching, two of the pictures including the back of her head with very long dark hair sprayed across her very white skin.

"I love how she does the contrast," whispered Sara. "The super dark background against the model's skin. That girl needed some sun!" she said with a giggle.

"When you said contrast, I thought you meant the soft hair against the hard muscles of her back. She is arching so hard—I find it very sexual, don't you?"

Sara blushed and broke eye contact with him. "Yes, well, Gellman is very sensual with her portraits. You know that's how she got her start, right?"

"No. I told you, I wanted you to teach me about her. I only knew her last name and saw a couple of pictures. I came here to see more," he lied.

"Well, she worked in the porn industry for a few years while she was trying to keep a roof over her head and working on her portfolio."

"Oh my," said Adam, feigning some sort of shock.

"Yeah. I'm not sure she is so sexual because of the time she spent in that industry, or if she went to that industry *because* she is so sexual, you know?"

"Yes, you are," he said quietly, looking deeply into her eyes.

"Yes I am, *what?*" she asked defensively.

"You *are* sure. Most women would never get anywhere near a movie set with actors having sex and doing all kinds of aberrant behaviors under the eyes of an entire film crew. If Lisa was comfortable enough to be around *that*, it is because she is very sexual herself. Judging by this picture, I'd say she goes both ways, wouldn't you?" He was staring deep into her eyes when he asked her.

Her mouth went dry. "I have no idea," she said quietly, and walked on to the next picture, obviously flustered by his comment.

The next picture was another nude, this time a partial male figure, again showing his tense back, shoulder and part of an extremely muscular arm. "Again, she shows figures straining—struggling perhaps," said Adam quietly to his new acquaintance.

"I never really looked at it like that, I guess," said Sara. "I always looked at her work more from a technical perspective. I am an amateur photographer myself. I have always admired the ways she uses her lens and lighting. I guess I never thought so deeply about the subjects. You seem to have an eye for the subtleties of her subjects."

"Subtle? I can practically hear the man screaming," he said quietly. He could practically taste the endorphins in the man's blood as he screamed in pain...he felt his teeth move.

She again moved on to the next picture. It was a kitten.

"Seems so out of place, no?" asked Adam.

She laughed. "Not really, the kitten is naked, too." He smiled. She had successfully lightened things up a bit. They continued their stroll down the gallery, and he listened to Sara explain some of the technical techniques that she found interesting. Adam could have cared less and tried his best not to stare at her carotid artery that was pumping so loud it was making him crazy. It was difficult to keep the animal inside sometimes. A hundred years ago he would have devoured her already—he *was* getting better with experience. He thought about the kitten for a split second and remembered eating one. It had been disgusting and made him vomit for quite some time.

The time passed and Sara looked down at her watch. "It's getting late," she said. "I should be getting ready to head home. It was nice meeting you, Adam," she said, extending her hand. Adam felt an uneasy feeling, a confusion he hadn't felt in this walking death after life. He wanted to continue to know more about her, but he also wanted to open her throat and suck every last ounce of blood out of her and feel and taste every bit of her. She was hesitating, waiting for him to ask for her number, ask her out, something?

"Perhaps you'd like to grab a drink?" he finally asked. It just sort of came out of his mouth.

"I don't know, I should probably get home. I have to work tomorrow." It wasn't a "no", she just needed a push.

"Oh, come on—just one. You won't be out late." He realized it was dinner hour and she would need to eat, (something he couldn't do in front of her.) He realized it would be bizarre for them to go out and "grab a bite" and then he *not* eat, so he quickly back-pedaled. "I'll tell you what—instead of a quick bite and a rush home because of work, what do you say we do something next Friday or Saturday night, when we can enjoy an evening out?"

She smiled and cocked her head, perhaps trying to decide if he was safe to go out with. He didn't *look* like a monster.

"Sure," she said with a smile. "That would be nice." She opened her purse and fished for a pen with which to write her phone number…

Eleven

The Village

Adam walked Sara out and saw her to a cab. Evidently, she didn't want to make the same long walk in the near-dark. Adam smiled his most charming smile and waved goodbye as she sped off in the taxi, and he began walking quickly, heading south down the long avenue. He walked faster and faster, feeling a rage building inside. He was hungry, that was true, but he was also angry. The woman had made him feel some type of actual emotions, something that hadn't happened since Renee, and he found it unnerving. The further he walked, the faster he went, and the angrier he became. What was it about *her*? He could almost feel his claws and teeth trying to come out, but concentrated as hard as he could to keep the animal inside.

The sun was setting behind the tall skyscrapers of New York, and

Adam walked until he was in Greenwich Village. He had been walking for over thirty minutes. Unlike humans, his legs felt no hint of being tired, although he was getting hungry. As he entered the smaller streets of Greenwich Village, he passed by a bar called the Slaughtered Lamb. It had a horror theme, and portrayed a werewolf hanging outside the bar. Inside, horror movies ran on small black and white televisions and grotesque statues and paintings decorated the popular bar. He smiled as he walked in and scanned the place. It was mostly young people, and they had wasted no time in starting to drink heavily. He spotted an obviously drunk young woman dressed appropriately in a style known as "Goth". Evidently, appearing dead was an actual fashion these days.

Her hair was dyed an unnatural black, while her makeup was extremely white with black lipstick. She had a lip ring, and eyebrow ring, and a nose ring. There were too many earrings to count. Black eye makeup finished her face along with her black "rouge" to hollow her cheek bones. It was a nice contrast to the black shirt, black jeans, black boots and black fingernails. Adam smiled and thought to himself, "She thinks she knows death?"

He moved through the crowd to get closer to her, intrigued by her makeup and attire, but most interested in her leopard skin fur coat. It was obviously fake, but it did look like fur, and Adam had every intention on sleeping on it this very evening. When he was next to her, he smiled and said, "I'd love to buy you a drink." He stared deep into her eyes, his own eyes now getting silvery and twinkling in the dim light of the bar. She was staring back into them, lost for a moment, and then responded with a heavy New York accent.

"Yeah? Patron tequila and a beer—how about that?"

"Sounds wonderful," he said, although he loathed the smell of tequila. It would affect her taste later on, he knew, but perhaps he could get other chemicals in her body to overpower the smoky taste it gave to blood. He ordered her drinks, and handed them to her.

"Where's yours?" she asked.

"Sweetheart, I am much too high to drink right now," he said in a slow soothing voice.

She threw back the shot quickly and washed it down with a swig from her cold beer. She appeared to really enjoy it, and Adam was feeling jealous. It was a very emotional day for him indeed.

"Yeah? You high? Your eyes *do* look kind of glazed," she said, staring into the silvery pools. "What ya' got?"

"On me? Oh, sorry, nothing *on* me. Too dangerous. The shit is just *too* good," he said, mocking her without her knowing it. "Such a sweet buzz…"

"Yeah? I bet. You live around here?" she asked, her own agenda starting to formulate.

"Not too far. Uptown a bit. What about you?"

"Right down the block. I love the fuckin' Village, ya' know?" She drank more of her beer, and Adam ordered another shot of tequila without asking her. He merely handed it to her and she threw it back. "So what kind of buzz you got going?" she asked.

"X and some snow," he said slowly, licking his lips at her. He had lived long enough to have seen and heard it all. This child, trying so hard to be cool, was a snack awaiting his invitation.

"X, huh? I love fuckin' on X. I can go all night." She leaned in closer, almost face to face. He looked at her and thought about her face. She might have been fairly pretty if not for the clown makeup and piercings. She had large breasts that would bleed well, and he could smell her pheromones kicking in, even with the smoke in the bar. Apparently, the 'No Smoking' sign was for show only.

"Me, too," he whispered, looking deeper into her eyes. His were now such a bright silver she couldn't stop looking into them.

"Man, you look wasted," she said, looking into his eyes of liquid mercury. Then she laughed, her own buzz kicking in. "I live right down the street," she said again.

"So you said. Maybe I could come visit," he said.

"Buy me another shot and beer and I'll take you home with me right now," she said with a slight slurr. She leaned in and rubbed her hands over his body. His body was hard and muscular.

"Damn—you this hard all over?" she said in her sexiest voice, her hand sliding down his pant leg.

He held her hand and whispered, "Not yet," then ordered her drinks. She drank them quickly, watching his silvery eyes twinkle while he licked his lips at her.

She looked at his tongue and whispered, "You just hold that thought, baby. I'm gonna' take that tongue for a ride."

"Let's go," he said, taking her by the hand and walking out of the bar with her, doing his best to keep his face low and in the dark. He was being much more careless than usual, but it had been an unusual day. That Sara woman had somehow upset him, and this poor woman was going to pay the price.

They left the bar, arm in arm, as he let her lead him down the block towards her apartment. They made an interesting couple—her in her wild Goth outfit and makeup, and he in his khaki slacks and dress shirt under a leather jacket. As they walked up the stairs to her studio, she whispered to him, "I like it a little rough," and scratched his hand with her fingernails.

He smiled, but said nothing.

She keyed her way into her apartment and screamed out *"Faye?"*, but there was no answer. "Good, my roommate's out. She'll be at her boyfriend's all night…"

Adam helped her with her fake leopard skin coat, and carefully placed it on the counter by the front door. He didn't want it soiled. He then placed his hand around her throat and leaned in to her, his other hand sliding over her large right breast, stopping to pinch and twist her nipple.

"Yeah…" she moaned. "That's it, baby. I like it rough." She reached down for the zipper of his slacks, but he took her hand and pulled it away hard, bringing it up behind her back enough to hurt.

"Yeah, baby…you gonna' give it to me hard?" she whined, leaning in to lick and nibble his neck. She was too drunk to realize how cold his skin was. He smiled to himself. He would soon be sucking her neck, too, just a little harder.

He picked her up and carried her to her bedroom. It was tiny, enough room for a bed and a bureau. There was a tiny television on top of a milk crate in the corner. He placed her on her feet gently, thinking that perhaps he would allow this one to give him a show for a moment. She seemed so enthusiastic, and he was still thinking about Sara. She would provide a nice distraction.

"Take off your clothes," he commanded.

"You don't want to take them off for me, baby?" she said, sticking out her black bottom lip in a fake pout. He reached out with lightning speed and ripped her lip ring off, splitting her lip and making her bleed.

"Fuck!" she screamed. "You *asshole!*" She put her hand over her lip and felt the blood. "You ripped my fucking lip!"

"You said you liked it rough," he replied slowly, and allowed his claws to extend only a few millimeters. He reached up and slashed open her blouse, her turquoise bra showing from underneath. The lace was pretty, and reminded him of the French whores from so long ago. He pushed her back on to the bed, and inhaled deeply. He smelled fear, and his hair tingled. He was on her quickly, tearing open her bra and sucking her breast into his mouth. She pushed back, but only a little. She was angry about her lip, but was turned on by his dominant nature. He sucked her nipple hard, feeling it harden in his mouth, and he heard her moan. He listened to the blood rushing faster in her veins, and could feel the animal inside him trying to get out.

"Soon…soon….but not yet," he told himself. He wanted to enjoy this for a moment. It was almost human. The woman was so turned on he could smell her sex. Pheromones and adrenaline were pumping in her veins. She would be delicious.

He stood up, towering above her in the tiny room. "Take everything off!" he bellowed, and she quickly complied, scared a little, but turned on by the whole scene. She had been beaten up by her sexual partners on more than one occasion, and was never one to complain about it. Sometimes it made her come even harder. She arched her back and ripped her own bottoms off, and as she arched, Adam thought back to the alabaster white skin of the arching girl in the photograph. Then he thought of Sara. A real woman he could never enjoy in the truest sense. The animal was coming out.

She threw off her bra and panties and laid back on the bed, spreading her legs shamelessly to show him her freshly shaven pubic mound. There was a tattoo of a dragon where her pubic hair had once been, and Adam found it ironic and wonderful. He leaned down between her legs and whispered, "You have a monster down there…" She didn't realize he meant himself. He pushed her thighs wide, her skin as white as the girl in the Gellman photo, and whispered, "Arch for me…"

The girl complied, now so turned on she was lost in her own lust.

She arched her back and squeezed her own breasts hard, pulling at her erect nipples and moaning as she pleaded with him to lick her. Adam licked across her sex slowly, smelling and tasting her hormones raging. Her blood was pounding in her veins so loud he couldn't believe that the neighbors couldn't hear it. His fangs and claws were sliding out, but he held himself together. He didn't want to lose control this time. He leaned into her thigh, seeing her blood rushing through her femoral artery. He slid his fangs in very slowly—gently even, and let her blood rush into his mouth.

"Oh gawwwwwd!" she moaned, arching her back even further as she squeezed her large breasts. She had no idea he had bitten clean through, instead only feeling him sucking so close to the parts that were needing to be sucked and licked. "Don't tease me anymore! I can't take it! Eat me!" she moaned.

He looked up at her and smiled, showing his bloody fangs. "You read my mind," he said, watching her eyes go wide as she saw his fangs, bloody from her thigh. She quickly tried to push away, but Adam was like lightning, and as strong as several men. He buried his face back in her crotch and bit so hard he completely severed her artery. The animal was out now, and he was no longer in control. His claws tore through her breasts as he pushed her down while sucking her blood violently through the large artery in her crotch.

She screamed terribly, but he leapt from her crotch to her throat burying his fangs in her throat and enjoying the spray of blood into his mouth. The taste of tequila was unpleasant, but mostly overpowered by sexual chemicals and adrenaline. Endorphins began to kick in as he tore her up, and he loved that special taste. It made him want to hurt her intentionally, wanting more of the chemical released when humans feel pain. He sucked her neck hard, and her kicking slowed as her life's energy vanished into his mouth. He felt her die, always the disappointing ending to his feast, but he slid down her chest and sucked blood from her breasts in an attempt to get something sexual from her. She was dead and the blood was mostly out of her, though. Her breasts no longer full of life and sexual pleasure.

Adam stood up and looked at her. She was pale. Very dead. Arched on the bed. "My God," he thought as a huge smiled crept across his bloody lips, "If I had a camera I could add her to the exhibit." A part of him wanted to call Sara and tell her to come right over and see what he had created for her, but he knew she wouldn't understand. He wiped his face and relaxed his hands, the talon-like claws sliding back into place. He knew he needed to get rid of the body. He *knew* it. He had learned a lot in over a century of murder—but he couldn't do it. He couldn't disturb the perfect scene he had made. He photographed it in his mind—saw it in black and white, and smiled. He grabbed her coat on the way out.

Twelve

Midtown North Precinct

onday afternoon started with the usual post-weekend madness. Weekends tended to be busier than midweek, and Roy worked a Thursday through Monday schedule most of the time. He walked in a little before three o'clock for a three to eleven shift.

"Morning Sergeant," mumbled one of the officers in his squad as he walked in for roll call. "Your phone's been busy today." Ruiz thanked him and headed over to his ancient wooden desk. It was probably the original desk from the 1950's when the precinct was built. The light for voicemail was flashing three at a time meaning he had three voicemails. The phone system was only a little newer than his desk.

The first message was from Captain Ammiano: "Hey, Roy. Just checking in from the lake. Fish are biting and the beer is cold—you'd hate it here. Was wondering if you had any luck with your missing person and I didn't want to bother you on your cell. Give me a call on my cell if anything breaks. Later."

The second message was from the medical examiner that had been studying the bones they found in the furnace" "Sergeant Ruiz, this is Doctor Valesi again. When you have some time, give me a call or stop by."

The third message was from his new friend Tim over in the sixth: "Hey, Pisano, its Rosetto. I had something come in last night. Give me a call on my cell ASAP. Ciao, baby."

Roy decided to call the doc first, since he might have something new to pass along to the captain. The doc insisted that he come down in person, so Roy hung up and headed down to the basement. He hated it down there.

"Whatcha got?" he asked as he walked in. The doctor was standing over a gurney with a cadaver on it, and Doctor Valesi covered it up with the green sheet.

"This way," he said, walking over to the metal drawers that held bodies. He pulled open a drawer and unzipped a cold black plastic body bag. Inside was a very dead looking female corpse. "This is another Jane Doe. She was found in the park about two months ago. We're getting ready to release the body for burial as a Jane Doe because we have no leads on her identification. No prints in the system, no dental records, nothing. She may have been an illegal immigrant. She looks Hispanic, so that's my best guess as to why we've got nothing on her. She had good teeth, unfortunately, so there aren't any cheap fillings to help me with my theory, but that's my best guess. Mexican Illegal. Maybe twenty years old. Anyway, there was no sexual assault. But death was by exsanguination. And she had teeth marks on her femur like your furnace victims." He made a scowl.

Roy looked up at the doctor. "Wait a minute. You're telling me this lady bled to death because something bit her?"

"I know, it sounds nuts. Quite honestly, Doctor Rogers and I discussed her in detail. Neither one of us has any real theories. There were no animal hairs anywhere. She had four other bite marks on her body consistent with a large predator of some type, but we have no idea what kind. We were keeping it quiet to avoid a panic in the park, but animal control was notified and they were patrolling, looking for large dogs or even a wolf. Hell, it could have been a tiger for all I know"

Roy folded his arms across his chest. "Dogs don't stuff people in furnaces, doc."

"I hear ya'. I can only tell you what I see. And in *this* case, what I *see* makes *no* sense, and I have nowhere to go with this. One of the gals up in missing persons spent three weeks on this poor woman and came up empty. We didn't know if it was a homicide or an animal attack. It wasn't until I matched the bite pattern to the bones from the furnace that I was sure it was the same animal."

"That's 100%?"

"Yup. Same bite," said the doctor.

Roy watched the doc zip up the bag. "Don't dispose of the body yet, okay? She'll keep for a while longer?"

"Yeah. We'll keep her on ice for you, but I am eventually gonna' need the space. This is a popular place, ya' know?"

"So I hear. Okay, thanks, doc. I'll talk to Captain Ammiano and get back to you."

Roy walked upstairs and went outside for some fresh air. He hated dead bodies, and knowing that it had been eaten by a dog—the same dog that some other sick bastard had used on three other victims was just too much. His cell phone rang.

"Ruiz," he said, walking out of the building.

"Hey, Pisano, you get my message?"

"Hey Tim. You were next on my list. I just came from the morgue. Got another DB with bite marks."

"Yeah, well so do I. And *this* one was in her *apartment*."

"Yeah? You got an ID? Witnesses?"

"We're working it now. I've ID'ed the girl. We're talking to her roommate who found her right now. *That* girl is going to need therapy for a while. Come over to the Six and I'll bring you over. Do *not* eat before you come."

"Oh shit," said Roy. "Not again."

He walked to the underground and hopped in his cruiser, heading quickly downtown.

Thirteen

The Village

Roy parked in the police garage and walked back up to find Tim. He wasn't hard to spot, right out in front of the precinct, on his cell phone drinking coffee. He waved his coffee at Roy when he spotted him and finished his call. Tim was a huge man. He stood about six feet tall, but was easily over three hundred and twenty-five pounds. He had thinning black hair that was slicked back over his head, and there was a handsome, gentle face under the extra chins and cheeks.

"Come on. I think we have a major break in the case."

"What have you got?" asked Roy, not sure he wanted to know.

"We can *walk* over. Son of a bitch was real close this time." They walked as Tim filled him in. "In all the missing persons files I've worked, we've hit dead ends. Any *bodies* we have followed up on, Jane

Doe cases that had weird causes of death, have *also* been dead ends. But *this* time, I've got something fucked up and no one is going to tell me otherwise." He stopped walking and turned to Roy, placing his large paw on Roy's shoulder. "Sergeant Ruiz, I work in Greenwich Village. I have some of the most fucked up characters on the planet in a few city blocks here, and in New York City, that's *saying* something. But *this* shit? This takes the cake."

"What happened?" asked Roy tentatively.

"I don't need a doctor to tell me the COD on this one. Some mutherfucker ate this chick."

Roy stopped in tracks. "*Ate* her?"

"Well, not the whole body. But it was like an animal was in there eating parts of her and, well…"

"What?"

"He drank her fucking blood!"

"He *what?*" asked Roy, wide eyed.

"There is not a drop of blood left in that woman's body up there. Oh, and she was into some Goth shit, so don't let that throw you off. Most of it is makeup."

"Goth shit?" asked Roy

"You gotta' come down to the Village more often, my friend. 'Goth', as in men and women that walk around dressed like they're dead. Black lipstick, nails, piercings, wild hair—you know…"

"I thought that was 'punk rock'?" asked Sgt. Ruiz.

"Holy shit, Roy. Get out from behind the desk, will ya? Punk went out in the eighties. Follow me."

The two of them walked up a flight of stairs to the second floor of a cheap apartment building. It was filthy outside, and not much better looking inside the hallway. They entered the crime scene, and the apartment itself, while tiny, was fairly neat. Two officers were inside finishing pictures and prints.

"You move her?" asked Tim.

"No, sir!" said an officer.

"Good. Roy, take a look."

Roy stepped into the tiny bedroom and cringed. A woman, white as a ghost, was spread wide on a bed. There were huge gaping wounds on her inner thighs, breasts, and throat. Her throat was ripped open so wide, Roy could see inside it.

"Oh, Jesus," he said, feeling sick. Then added to no one in particular, "I know—he isn't a suspect."

"Whatever did this to her went right for the arteries in her crotch and neck. Carotid and femoral. I'm no doctor, but I have enough first aid training to know *that* much. There is very little blood anywhere in this room, and *look* at her wounds. This place should be a swimming pool. And judging by her face, I'd have to say she was alive when this happened."

It was true. Roy looked at her face, and makeup or not, her expression was frozen in absolute terror. Her eyes were wide open, as well as her mouth. It looked like she was still screaming.

"How much you want to bet the bites match your furnace victims?"

"And the chick in the morgue."

"Yeah, you never told me—what's the deal with her?"

"She's a Jane Doe. Maybe an illegal immigrant. A total dead end. But she's been down in the morgue for weeks. The doc said they thought she was attacked by a dog or something in Central Park. Truthfully, I think they didn't have a clue, and since no one was asking about her, they were just going to put her in the "I have no fucking idea file' and move on. When Doc Valesi saw the bite marks on the furnace victims, it rang a bell and he called me on this DB down in the fridge."

"Jesus H. Christ," said Tim under his breath. "We've got some lunatic that thinks he's a fucking werewolf running around the city eating people."

"Let's hope the roommate can give us something. And hey—thanks for calling me on this."

Tim opened his arms. "Hey, Piazan! We're in this together, right?"

"Yeah. And at least if this thing attacks me when I'm with you, he'll go for you. You're a bigger meal."

"Thanks a fucking lot. And I thought we were friends."

· · ·

Roy got back to the Midtown North Precinct after four-thirty. By the time he got there, his light was blinking on his phone again. He sat down at his desk and rubbed his face. It had been a seriously messed up day, and it was only just starting. The message was Captain Ammiano, and Roy called him back and gave him every detail of what had happened thus far.

"Jesus, Roy. I can't leave the city for two days and you got werewolves and shit running around the city?"

"It's not funny, man. I'm tellin' ya', this is not a normal crime scene."

"When did you ever see a 'normal' homicide?" asked the captain.

"I'm serious, captain. Tim—the cop in Six, he and I are matching up some cases, and I swear, this whack-job has been at this a long time. I think we have a serial killer running around the Apple that makes Dahmer and Manson look like choirboys."

The captain let out a long sigh. "Okay, I'll be in tomorrow."

"I thought you were out for two weeks?"

"Yeah, well…couple of days of fishing and drinking beer upstate was fine, but it's so fucking quiet up here I'm gonna' lose my mind. I'll come down and help find your lunatic. And don't say serial killer to anyone else, okay?"

"Yeah, okay. Thanks, cap. Call me when you get back."

Roy called Tim, who answered quickly.

"Hey, Tim, it's Roy. My captain is coming back from vacation early to help with this case. I am going to grab my lieutenant as soon as I get off the phone with you. What say we have a meeting, and we bring all of the missing persons cases and unsolved homicides or Doe cases with us? Maybe try and map this thing out."

"I'm way ahead of ya', Pisano. I had one of my guys spend an entire day with a city map pushing color-coded thumbtacks. The attacks, the missing persons last known addeys, recovered DB's that were still open files—all of this shit is totally random. But I did have something really weird come up today. I am thinking it has to be a mistake, but this case is so bizarre already, that who knows?"

"Whatcha' got?" asked Roy.

"Well, we got some prints in the apartment that didn't match the two girls or the roommate's boyfriend. Truthfully, there were a lot of prints in there, and from what the roommate says, there were guys in and out of her roommates place all the time. She was into some kinky shit. We found a bag of sex toys in her room that made me blush. Hell, I don't even know what some of the stuff is used for…"

"And you told me I should get out more?" joked Roy.

"Really. Anyway, this chick liked it rough I guess, and apparently had plenty of takers on her offers. There were no less than thirty sets of prints in there. However…" he paused. "We did get a perfect print in the girl's blood off of the counter near the front door."

"You guys work fast," said Roy, impressed with what he was hearing so far. Unlike television shows that solved cases in thirty minutes with forensics that gave instant information, in the real world, evidence took weeks or months.

"My little cousin works in the lab. I told him this was a possible serial killer and pushed it way to the top of the pile."

"Your *little* cousin? Like under three hundred?"

"Fuck you very much. No, like he's twenty-seven and smart as hell. He did the print work himself, and the kid is very thorough and very good, which is why I am so confused about this."

"About what?"

"That print appeared at another unsolved homicide."

"Yeah? That's *great*! Our first real lead!" said Roy with sudden energy.

"Not so great. That case is from 1959."

Roy sat and let that sink in. He did the math. A murder case that was fifty-two years old. "So our killer is like, seventy years old?"

"Well, unless he started as a very young teenager, he's at least sixty-five."

"You're right, that *is* weird. A sixty-five or seventy year old man is going to have to be in pretty good shape to be attacking young women and carrying bodies around."

"Unless he has help," said Tim, thinking out loud.

"Yeah, along with his pet tiger or wolf or whatever the fuck he walks around with. How the hell could anyone not see some crazy old guy with a fucking lion on a leash?"

"New York City, baby. Who knows? But this case is getting weirder by the minute. Tell you what—when your captain gets back, you call me, or have him call me. I want to put together a task force on this right away. I am speaking to the chief later today, and I am using the term 'serial killer' when I see him. He's gonna' go ape-shit, but I don't care. I am convinced this shit is all related. Jesus, Roy—what if this guy really has been at this since 1959?"

What if he had been at it since 1806?...

Fourteen

Adam

Adam awoke nude, lying on top of a fake fur coat that smelled like cigarette smoke, cheap perfume, and spilled alcohol. These were smells he didn't normally enjoy, but knowing it came from his last kill made him want to roll around in it the way a dog rolls in the grass, experiencing every smell. He could still feel her warmth. Her blood still warmed his beating heart. He inhaled the coat deeply and felt a sexual urge between his legs. It had been decades since he had fornicated, and until seeing Sara, had never actually missed it, that urge having been replaced by the lust for blood that was *so* much more powerful. He rolled on his stomach and rubbed himself against the coat, breathing it in as he looked at the black and white picture in his head—that woman, so pale and white, with her black lipstick and makeup and hair...such a beautiful image. He wished had taken a picture and snuck it into the Gellman exhibit. Perhaps no one would even notice it wasn't Gellman's herself. He wished he could have shown Sara. He was unconsciously humping the coat as he thought of her, still feeling warm and satisfied after such a lovely meal.

He drifted in and out of his aroused state, between sleep and dreams and flashbacks of his ancient life. He remembered another woman he found interesting back in France. How long ago was it now? He remembered her beautiful dress, the bright colors, her strong perfume and body odors. They didn't bathe nearly as much back in those days as they did today, and a human body seemed much more intoxicating back then, particularly the French whores who would have sex several times an evening for days at a time between baths. That one young woman—a girl, really, Renee—she had been beautiful. She had approached Adam; he was still Olmer then, near the docks. Olmer had decided to travel to America at the time, ahh—he remembered, it must have been back in 1861 or so when the Americans were still slaughtering each other. It was at that time, when he was living near the seaport at Normandy, that he met Renee.

That first time he met her came right after he had lost control and let the animal out. He had eaten and drank four large sailors the evening before, and then tossed their remains to the crabs at the wharf. That was the first time he had ever tested his strength to such a degree. He was in a dark mood, having seen how much fun the sailors seemed to be having drinking and eating and fornicating with the French whores, and he was an outsider looking in. The more he saw, the louder the music became, and the more he could hear the blood pumping in the strong mens' hearts. He picked a fight with a group of drunken sailors outside near one of the boats. It was so late that night that no one else was around. He goaded them into attacking him, and then proceeded to tear all four strong men apart. He ate and drank them until he was so full he was vomiting blood back up, only to drink more and rip off huge chunks of flesh. He wanted so much to be able to drink in the bar—to eat a steak from an animal—have sex with a beautiful woman and sleep with her afterwards. He was *angry*.

After he had eaten himself to nausea, he dropped the bodies into the water and returned home to sleep it off. The next evening, he awoke feeling stronger and more alive than ever before in his afterlife. He followed the sound of music from his small room at an inn back to the pubs along the water, and that was where he saw Renee. She was so young and innocent looking. A fresh faced child beneath the heavy whorish makeup and large white wig worn by women in her trade. He approached her and smiled, and she put her arms around his neck and kissed him before even saying hello. He could taste wine on her lips, and it smelled pleasant. He breathed her in, smelling sex and alcohol and sweat, not all of it hers. She was intoxicating to him, and her young clear voice was musical. Perhaps it was because of the energy he felt from such a large feast the night before, the fact that he couldn't possibly eat or drink her, that he felt something "different" with her.

He listened to her flirt and let her kiss his face and neck, until she finally asked him if he'd like a fuck. He smiled and asked her to join him back at his room. She pouted and explained she wouldn't be allowed at any "proper" inn, but that she had a room upstairs in the pub "just for their purposes". He let her lead him up the stairs, where she stopped only once to ask him if he had five francs. He pulled out twenty and pressed them into her hand, and her smile was contagious.

"Does Messieurs wish to stay a long time?" she asked with a coy smile.

"Indeed," he answered, and followed her to her small room. He entered the room and inhaled deeply. She had been a busy beaver indeed in this very room. "How many tonight?" he asked her.

"You are my *very* first," she lied. He smiled and didn't bother to comment. He sat on a small three-legged stool in the corner of the tiny room. The only furniture was a small bed and a counter with a wash basin and towel. He watched her slowly undress, allowing the heavy dress to fall off around her ankles, and was pleased to see her naked beneath. She knelt before him and pulled off his tall black boots. He allowed her to remove his clothes, standing when she asked, so she could unbutton his pants and make him naked like her. Then she went back to her knees in front of him and began doing something that no other woman had had ever done for him before. He spoke Prussian for the first time in years as she expertly worked his manhood, making it feel very alive indeed for the first time in over fifty years.

"Mon Dieu," she whispered, as he grew. She looked up at him. "It is so big."

"Do you like it?" he asked. Before dying and being reborn, he had known only one other woman, a farm girl in his village that he fucked before going off to war. It had been hurried and secretive, and all too quick.

She squeezed his shaft and worked it up and down. "I love it. I want it inside me," she cooed. They made love that night like two humans, and Olmer actually lay with her after several hours of lovemaking. She was amazed at his strength and ability to keep going, even after she had lost count of her own orgasms. She finally begged him to stop before she couldn't walk, and she passed out with a large smile on her face. Olmer had watched her fall asleep and listened to her heart beat and breathing slow as she drifted off. To his own amazement, he was satisfied not to drink her blood. He was still full from the evening before, and was enjoying the warmth and smell of her body. He closed his eyes and listened to her blood pumping, wondering what she tasted like, but controlling his urge for the first time ever.

She awoke the next morning and smiled at him. "You were amazing," she said. "I will give you a free one if you wish."

He smiled, and she surprised him by getting out of bed and pulled a bedpan from under their bed. "Excuse me for a moment," she said, and squatted over it to urinate in front of him. When she was finished, she covered it and slid it under the bed. "Oh, I'm sorry," she said, "Did you need to relieve yourself as well?"

"Only with you," he smiled, and she climbed back into bed to begin again.

Olmer stayed with her for four days and nights. He might have stayed forever and cancelled his plans for America altogether, but on the fifth night, the animal came out. She was, as he had guessed, the most delicious thing he had ever eaten.

· · ·

ADAM OPENED HIS EYES WITH a start. He looked around the room and remembered where he was. New York. 2011 A.D. Renee was long dead. Eaten by him. He looked down at the fur coat and was surprised to see that he had ejaculated all over it. He hadn't done that since… he couldn't even remember. His thoughts turned immediately to Sara.

Fifteen

Sixth Precinct

It was Wednesday morning. Roy's day off. But if the Captain could come back from vacation, then he and Lieutenant Joe could give up a Wednesday. The three of them had gathered up their files and drove downtown into the Village for a special meeting with Tim and several of his officers. Chief Schrieffer was going to be sitting in as well. They entered the Precinct carrying boxes full of files, and found the conference room full of cops, including Tim and the Chief. After introductions and pleasantries, the eleven of them sat down at a large conference table.

Tim began the meeting. "Thank you for taking the drive downtown, and thanks to the chief for allowing us to set up this special task force. We are still not officially calling this a serial killer, but we are looking at a possible connection between unsolved murders and missing persons cases dating back several decades." He looked at the chief. (See? He was playing nice and not saying the obvious, that some whackjob had been killing and eating people all over New York for fifty years.)

At this point, I'd like to turn the meeting over to Heather Connell, who will catch us up on some of the forensic evidence she has put together for us. Heather is from here in the Sixth, but has worked with the State Police and the feds on some very large cases. Heather—please..."

The woman stood up and picked up a rolled up map, which she tacked to the wall. She was in her forties, and a no-nonsense type of professional. She was also the only woman in the room.

"Gentlemen, this is a map of Manhattan showing every unidentified DB in red, every last known missing person location in blue, and every murder of 'unsolved origin' in black."

"What's unsolved origin? Open files?" asked one of the men.

"Unknown weapon. The case may have been closed, but it was never solved and the cause of death was undetermined at the time. Quite frankly, these are most likely victims that were bitten and sucked dry like your apartment victim, but no coroner was going to sign off on *that*."

"So this has happened before a bunch of times and no one said anything about it, like, 'hey—I think we have some kind of wild animal eating people in New York'?" Asked Roy incredulously.

"Pretty much. One of the files was from here in the Sixth. The cop still works here in records. He's got thirty years in and is past retirement age, but he's so good no one bothers him. Anyway, I went to go see him. I asked him if he remembered the case. He turned white. No kidding. He actually looked sick. He told me a long story which I will abridge for you. Basically, he and his partner found a woman that he said looked half eaten. She had no ID, and they had zero leads. His description of what he saw was so detailed that I didn't need pictures. It made an impression on him, know what I'm sayin'? Anyway, I asked him what happened to the case. It was worked for months, no leads, no nothing, and eventually just put aside. It was ruled a homicide, and she bled to death, but the coroner said that animals must have worked the body after she died. The cop said no way. He says the bites were the cause of death, but the examiner at the time is dead for ten years, and I can't ask him about it."

"Why was the cop so sure it was the cause of death?" asked one of the men.

Tim jumped on him before Heather could answer. "For those of you not present at the last crime scene, the one we call 'Goth Girl', you wouldn't understand—but let me tell you, looking at that victim, there was zero doubt about the cause of death. The killer bit her, sucked her dry of her blood, and ate a few bites of her here and there. He also tore her up pretty good with some type of claw device. She had what looked like tiger-paw claw marks on her body. It didn't even look like a human attack—more like an animal."

Heather chimed in. "That's exactly what Charlie down in records said. That it looked like a wild animal attacked her and killed her. The only reason they knew it wasn't an animal was because a witness called the police when the woman started screaming. A man was seen running from the scene. He had two legs, two arms and a head. It was human. The scene sure didn't look like it, though."

One of the officers raised his hand. "Excuse me. When you say, 'he sucked her dry of her blood', you mean he drained it with something, right? I mean, he didn't drink a whole body-worth of blood, right?"

Heather and Tim looked at each other and made a face that read: "Your guess is as good as mine". She answered the question first. "Look. As far as we know, he could have used a weapon that was made to look like teeth marks or claw marks. He could have drained the fluids with a hose. Anything is possible, I suppose. But the coroner's report, and the last one on Goth girl was very thorough, did not mention any marks that might have come from tools. In fact, when I spoke with the doctor, he was pretty specific about the teeth marks matching other 'bite victims'. He refers to them as bite victims, not tool marks or sharp weapon marks. As far as I am concerned, this guy is eating and drinking human tissue and blood."

"But an entire bodies-worth of blood? Isn't that impossible? I mean, the guy would puke, wouldn't he? There was very little blood in the crime scene photos I saw," asked another cop. "What human could drink that much blood, even if he was crazy, and keep it down?"

"Maybe he takes it with him for later? Drains it into a bag or something?" asked the first cop.

"I have no idea, and right now, that is not our focus. We have to assume, for the time being, that we are dealing with a male subject, approximately sixty-five to seventy years old, who is capable of biting, clawing and eating other human beings in order to ingest their tissue and fluids. That about sum it up, Tim?" asked Heather.

"I'm glad *you* said that," he replied. "If *I* had said that, I know they'd all think I was crazy."

"Sixty-five to seventy years old?" screamed one of the cops.

"Yes, I know that sounds as bizarre as the rest of it, but the fingerprints are a match to an open murder case from 1959. I double checked and tripled checked the prints. They are a match. And unless this guy breaks the rules of 'no two prints alike', he is the same killer."

"That's ridiculous," said one of the officers under his breath.

Heather folded her arms and looked at the floor for a moment before speaking. "Look. I have worked some pretty unusual cases. So has Tim and so have most of you. New York City gives you a sampling of everything. But honestly, I have never seen *anything* like this. This breaks every rule of logic there is. I have decided to just examine the facts for what they are each time something comes in. Don't filter it with your brain for being logical or normal or fitting into any pattern you have ever seen, okay? Just look at it with an open mind and try to stay sharp and focused. Just gather evidence and let the picture come into focus."

Tim rubbed his face. "Listen up, everyone. What Heather just said can't be overstressed. You are all experienced investigators. You've been through a lot of cases—seen a lot of crazy shit, pardon my French. You need to think outside the box on this one. And you need to keep this investigation entirely confidential."

At that point, the chief stood up and everyone shut up. "Gentlemen, and lady, this case is going to be worked by the people in this room and only in this room. We are not releasing any information until we have more to go on, and we are not calling this a serial killer yet. While this is certainly starting to look like a connected string of incidents, I personally find it hard to believe that a cannibal killer can stay under the radar for fifty years while eating victims every week or two. If one word of this investigation leaks to the press, I will find out who it is, and that person will be walking a beat in Harlem until the end of time. Are we all understood? Well?"

There was a room full of "Yes, sirs."

The chief grunted and continued. "Midtown North's Captain Pat Ammiano will be lead along with Sixth Precinct's Captain Tim Rosetto.

Lieutenant Alexander and Sergeant Ruiz from Midtown North will also be working with the rest of you from Sixth. I don't give a rat's ass who finds this guy. We are all working together, and regardless of *who* finds it from *whichever* precinct, the collar goes to everyone in the room from this special task force. I want everyone's full cooperation and sharing of information. If you can't check your ego at the door, you can use it to walk out of this room now." He looked at each man, one at a time, then back to Heather. "Ms. Connell will liaison between you and the labs. She will be working with Dr. Valesi and the lab techs downstairs here. Any questions?"

"We authorized for overtime?" asked Tim, an efficient manager already thinking about his budget.

"I have some Homeland Security money set aside for a rainy day. It's raining. Do whatever you need to do. Catch this sick fuck before he kills somebody else. That's all from me, good luck," said the Chief, and with that he left.

Sixteen

Adam's First Date

Adam waited three painful days before deciding to call Sara. He didn't want to appear too eager and scare her off, and didn't want to wait too long and have her forget him. He hadn't ever been in this situation before, and found it interesting and somewhat exciting. He tried to remember what it was like when he was alive. Had he ever had a girlfriend? Was there anyone that ever made him feel something special inside? He couldn't recall. He only remembered fumbling clumsily with that one farm girl who was a bit older than he, and was interested in "sending him off to war like a man". They had fornicated quickly in a barn, banging away in the hay no better than the farm animals. It had taken them longer to get their clothes off than it did for him to finish, something she wasn't very happy about.

Then, of course, his thoughts turned back to Renee. He might have even felt something like love for her. Before he partially ate her and sucked her dry of all of her blood, of course. He was sorry about that, in a way. She had been one of the tastiest and most satisfying meals he had ever experienced. He just wished he could have held off and enjoyed her physical company longer. He truly enjoyed the feeling of having sex with her. He enjoyed watching her orgasm, with all of the heightened smells and sounds and body heat. It was certainly the closest he had ever felt to being alive again since that fateful night in the woods of Jena. If only he could have kept the animal inside. How long could it have lasted?

He thought of Sara and wondered. What if she was different than the rest? What if he had found a human that he wanted to be with? Perhaps he could make *her* like *himself*, and they could be together forever? That was a new thought. He had never considered that. How would he even do it? How did that undead thing infect him? He crouched in a corner of his room, his back against the wall, and wrapped his arms around his knees with his chin on them. It was the same position he had been in when he tried to disappear from the sound of screaming that night in the woods. He closed his eyes and remembered the sounds of that creature that made him what he was now. It was slashing and slurping and munching while those crude men screamed and begged for mercy. He felt sad again. He missed being alive at that moment, and that made him angry again. Almost *any* emotion he felt triggered anger, and let the animal out. He fought the urge to let it come out. Now was not the time or place. He was in his home. He needed to be careful.

Adam thought about Sara's smile and her twinkling eyes. The bitch was alive. She was teasing him. She was flaunting it at him. He fought the claws coming out and said "no" quietly. She was doing no such thing. He was jealous, simple as that. She was the picture of "life" itself—so bubbly and happy and energetic. Yes—that was the word, energetic. And then he remembered how he had gorged himself on the sailors the night before he met Renee. That huge meal had kept the animal inside for three days, and allowed him to be around her almost like a human. She never knew he wasn't human—well, at least not until his fangs and claws slid out and he ripped her to pieces as he sucked every drop of fluid out of her. But before that—he had enjoyed three wonderful days with her. And now Sara. How long could he last with her? Perhaps if he gorged himself, he could be around her safely, without succumbing to his animal inside.

He stood, feeling energized. He had a plan. He would arrange an evening to meet her, and prior to seeing her, he would gorge himself and keep himself under control. He actually smiled, and felt almost human. He dressed and walked out of his building to purchase a disposable cell phone. He had never had use for a phone, and didn't want his name on any phone bills anyway. This was a minor inconvenience, but he smiled again at himself, thinking that he was certainly joining the twenty-first century now. He would have a phone. How charming.

Adam purchased the disposable cell phone and walked back to his apartment, watching and smelling the crowds on the street, allowing his appetite to build. He felt nervous as he dialed. It was wonderful to feel so human, even if the anger was always present in the background as a reminder that he was *not* human, and would never be human again. He pushed the anger away. The phone rang twice, and then her crisp happy voice answered and said, "Hello?"

"Hello Sara," he said calmly. He felt an urge to reach through the phone and rip open her throat. He needed to feel her blood spurt into his mouth and taste every nuance of her being. He exhaled slowly and fought it off. "It's Adam Priest," he said softly. "From the gallery."

"Adam! I was *sure* you had tossed my number! Nice to hear your voice. How *are* you?"

She was so sweet it was angering. She must taste delicious. She must. He exhaled slowly and pushed the claws back in. "I'm fine, Sara. Truthfully, I have been thinking about our day in the gallery. It was a nice day for me. A treat, really."

"Aww, that's so *sweet*," she said. She sounded sincere, as corny as it was. "It was a nice exhibit, although I don't suppose I'll ever look at her work the same way again." He could almost hear her smiling.

"Yes, well, perhaps you moved from the technical aspect into a truer appreciation of what she was trying to convey."

"I'm sure," she replied.

"When we last spoke, I had asked if you might care to join me for an evening when you didn't have to work the next day. Friday or Saturday, if you are free?"

"Well, I hadn't heard from you, and I really didn't think you would call, so I made plans for the weekend," she said with hesitation in her voice.

"I see," he said. It came out sounding sad, and as he heard himself, he could feel anger again at trying to be so fucking human.

"It's no big deal. Let me make a phone call and see what I can do. I'll call you right back, okay?" she asked.

He panicked for a moment. He didn't even know his number. "Um, sure, that would be fine…"

"Okay—your number is in my cell, I'll call back in a couple." The phone went dead, like Adam Priest, and he sat quietly, feeling totally out of sorts. If he had a heart, it might even be pounding with what? Nerves? He smiled. He *did* feel almost human. *Amazing*. What if he *could* have her join him in his "forever"?

He crouched back into the corner of his room again, arms wrapped around his knees, posed almost bat-like—the way he had spent that night in Jena. He sat and watched the phone, his head cocked awaiting the ring. His thoughts drifted over a sea of time. He could hear Renee laughing. Then screaming in shock and horror, her face showing such betrayal, as he opened her throat with his fangs and enjoyed the hot spray of her oxygenated blood. It was foamy—fine champagne. The phone rang and snapped him back to 2011.

"Hello Sara," he said.

"Hi again. I blew off my friends and told them I had a hot date. I *assume* you are a hot date," she said with a cheerful laugh that made him smile.

"I will try my very best."

"Anyone who likes Gellman and can teach me about my favorite photographer can't be all bad," she joked.

"I can't be all bad," he repeated, wondering what she would look like torn open and bleeding with her entrails strewn about her body. "It's settled then. I shall see you Friday night? You need only give me your address."

Seventeen

Thursday – Taskforce Begins

Captains Ammiano and Rosetto had assigned each officer from their two precincts a box of very old cases to begin examining. While none of the reports came right out and said that any recovered body had been "eaten" or "drained of blood", there were a few that described "scenes of particular violence" where the body had been mutilated. A few of the files had pictures, and once you started looking for it, you realized that even though the bodies may have been violently torn up, there was very little blood in any photo. Sloppy police work. You'd think *someone* would have noticed.

The majority of cases they looked at were just missing persons files, and when it came to hookers and illegal aliens, there wasn't much to go on. There were *boxes* of old files like that, and most of them were women. The two captains discussed at great length the problem they faced in trying to run a stakeout for a cannibal killer that looked like somebody's grandfather without running counter to the chief's instructions of secrecy. When they called him and explained their situation, asking for officers to be notified of their vague description of a possible serial killer so they could run a city-wide manhunt, they were told not to get overzealous. While "Goth Girl" *had* been brutally murdered, the chief reminded them she was *also* into some kinky shit and was very promiscuous. There was no guarantee that she could be linked to any other missing person case. When they hung up with the chief, they were pissed.

"What's his problem?" asked Tim. "We are painting the picture pretty clearly of some whacked out homicidal lunatic, and the chief is afraid of bad press? This is ridiculous."

Pat sat back and frowned. "The chief is still walking funny from the ass reaming he got from the Mayor a few months back. A couple of DBs had turned up related to some gang activity, the chief released a statement about it, and the papers ran two months of stories about 'gangs running midtown'. It killed tourism for part of the summer, and the mayor's favorite restaurant near the crime scene closed down. The mayor was *pissed* about that—God forbid he might miss a meal, the fat fuck—no disrespect to you—and made the chief's life miserable. So now the chief's walking on eggshells."

Tim made a face. "You mean to tell me we can't warn the city because the mayor's favorite restaurant closed down? Are you fucking kidding me?"

"Until we can prove that we have multiple murders all committed by the same guy, we can't make a public statement. Period."

· · ·

AFTER ADAM HUNG UP WITH Sara, he spent the rest of the afternoon trying to recall how he came to be. How was it that the thing that made him didn't kill him? It was so long ago. At times, it seemed like yesterday, but more often than not, the sea of time had clouded so many of his memories. He remembered the battle itself and the days leading up to the route at Jena. He remembered the horrible night of the attack. But what had the thing done to him *specifically*? He sat in the corner again, arms wrapped around his legs and chin on his knees, and tried to remember. The thing had bitten his throat. He remembered the smell of its breath. He closed his eyes and concentrated. The thing had exhaled hard into his lungs…had spit blood into his open wound. Maybe *that* was it. It had *breathed* its life into him and mixed their bloods. Maybe that is how it infected him. Could *he* do it *too*? Did he posses that ability? If Sara was indeed someone he would want to make into his permanent company, could he even do it?

He would need to practice. But on whom? What if it worked, and he created another being like himself that he couldn't control? It could be disastrous. He rocked back and forth on his feet. He was lost in thought when he heard a bird singing outside, and then had a thought. Perhaps he could try it on an animal first, rather than a human? He decided he would try.

Wednesday had faded into Thursday, and he was still in the same spot in the corner of his apartment. Once he had come to the conclusion that he would try his experiment on an animal, he became animated, and Adam left his apartment in somewhat of a hurry. It was approaching darkness and he had his first date the next night. There was much to do before then. He needed a huge meal to keep him calm on his date, and he needed an animal subject for his attempt at "procreating".

Adam hustled off into the darkening streets of New York and decided to venture a bit further than usual. He knew he had been careless in Greenwich Village, and wouldn't make the same mistake twice, especially if was going to take several victims at once. Where could he go that he could find several strong male victims that no one would notice missing? He decided it was time for a subway trip.

Adam hopped on a subway heading uptown, with no particular place in mind. He just figured he would know it when he spotted it. He kept heading north, changing trains, looking for the oldest and dirtiest subway lines. As the crowd on the train grew smaller and rougher looking, he smiled. When four short, heavily muscled and tattooed Latino males got on the train wearing red bandanas, swearing profusely and looking menacing, he knew he was getting close. He looked at the four of them and could smell their sweat. He could hear their hearts pounding louder than the clack of the subway wheels. One of them pulled a knife and carved his name in a seat, not caring who saw him vandalizing city property. They cursed and joked and occasionally looked towards Adam, in his neat clothing. He wondered how long it would take before they got around to him.

Two stops after they got on, they hopped off, and Adam got off at the same stop, exiting out a different door. He stood on the platform, which was empty except for the four gangbangers and himself. He smiled and walked up the stairs to the street above. The neighborhood looked like one of the cities he vaguely remembered in war torn Europe some sixty years ago. Empty, burnt out buildings and garbage was everywhere. He walked quickly, listening to the men behind him trying to whisper about him. He heard them, and he smiled. He looked around him. Most of the streetlights were broken, and it was dark and void of life in this part of the city. He smiled broadly when one of the men behind him screamed over at him in Spanish. He kept walking. The man repeated himself, this time in English.

"Hey! You *lost* futherfucker?"

He stopped and turned to face the approaching "crew". One of them slid a knife from his pocket. It was the same one that had carved his initials in the seat.

"I *said*, you lost motherfucker? What you doin' in this neighborhood, pussy?"

Adam smiled and stopped walking. He inhaled deeply and felt his hair starting to stand on his arms. It was like electricity pumping through him as his claws started to tingle under his skin. His mouth felt full again, as razor sharp fangs slowly began to extend from their hidden slots.

He stared at them, his eyes going silver and shimmering in the dark street.

"You got off at the wrong stop, heffe," snarled one of the men. "You in our neighborhood without permission. You gotta pay a tax." He laughed at his great joke.

"*Everybody* gotta pay a *tax*, pussy," said one of the others, finding his fellow punk very amusing.

Adam inhaled again, smelling adrenaline. He wanted a fight, not just a meal. He wanted to taste the testosterone, the adrenaline and the endorphins when he hurt them so badly. He goaded them.

"I think you will all pay *me* a tax. *Each* of you. Before I tear you all into little pieces."

They kept walking closer, fanning out around him as they approached. "You a tough guy, huh?" said one with a smile. "You better have a gun."

One of them pulled a thirty-eight from his waist band. "*I* got a gun, pussy. *You* got a gun?" He aimed it at Adam's chest. "Huh? You bring a gun, pussy? Or you just gonna' give me all your money and beg me not to kick your fuckin' ass…"

Adam smiled, his fangs now sliding down into position. He closed his hands to hide the long razor talons that now extended a full inch from his fingertips. He could open a can with them.

"No gun," he said quietly. "I'd rather use my hands. Wouldn't all of you? Pussies…"

The one in the center snapped at that, and ran straight for him. Adam let the animal out. He slashed the man's throat open with one swift arm motion, and the man dropped, spraying blood and clutching his open throat.

"He got a fuckin' knife!" yelled one of the others, and the one with the gun fired at Adam's chest. The slug went straight through Adam's chest, and Adam sprung at him like a leopard, snapping his arm like a twig, making him drop the gun. He brought his other hand around the man's leg and cut his hamstring completely through to the bone, dropping the man to the ground. An attacker jumped at him from behind, but Adam's reflexes were like lightning, and he spun around and brought his hand down so hard on the man's shoulder he could hear the clavicle snap. The last man standing was the one with the knife, which he shoved as hard as he could into Adam's stomach. He twisted it and snarled at Adam.

"Take that, motherfucker!" he yelled, then pulled it out to attack again with it. Adam opened his mouth and showed his fangs, howling with rage. He leapt at the man and used both hands to grab the man by the face, pulling his head back to expose his throat. He sunk his mouth into the man's neck and growled as the man's carotid sprayed into his mouth. He sucked deeply, feeling the power rushing into his body. The man gurgled and dropped like dead weight, and Adam could hear two of the others trying to get up. He dropped the one in his mouth and turned on the other two.

One of the thugs was still holding the back of his leg, trying to stand, but having difficulty moving, his leg muscle completely severed, causing extreme agony. Adam could smell the endorphins and hear his blood pumping. He moved so fast the two men still alive both screamed in terror. He was on the man, his mouth on the man's throat in a second, ripping and tearing through muscle tissue and arteries. The hot blood sprayed in his mouth and he sucked so hard the man's arteries collapsed in his neck and chest. He dropped that one and turned to the last, who was now up and trying to run, his shoulder broken in several places, but his legs moving as fast as he could. Adam could smell the fear and pain and feel blood beating his own dead heart. He hadn't felt so alive in decades. Adam ran the man down in a matter of seconds and pulled him to the ground.

Adam jumped on the man's back and used his talons to grip his pray. The man howled as the claws shredded his back, and Adam sunk his teeth into the man's shoulder, tearing out a huge chunk of muscle tissue. He didn't want to kill this one too quickly. He wanted the man's blood to be full of as many chemicals and tastes as possible. He slowly sucked and began chewing on his victim, bones cracking under the gurgling sounds of the creature feeding. The man was trying to scream, but no sound would come out now as shock took over. Adam stopped for a moment, lest he kill him too quickly, and dragged him back to the others. One was already dead, and the other two were close. He saw blood flowing and grew angry at the waste. He let go of the one he had been enjoying, and grabbed the one closest to death before his meal was ruined. He bit through the man's shirt and ripped out a piece of his chest, then used his hands to open the man's chest and pull out the heart while it still beat. The man who was still alive had to witness this creature eat his friend's heart, slurping and sucking it dry.

Adam went back and forth between the three that were still alive, enjoying the subtle differences in their blood chemistry, now completely lost in his blood lust. He ate chunks of flesh, knowing they would make him sick, but not caring. He tore the bodies apart, breaking bones, ripping tissues and organs, and sucking back so much blood he felt like a tick on a dog.

Fifteen minutes later, Adam was still crouching on the ground, in the middle of what had been four men. His teeth had bits of flesh stuck in them, his silvery eyes turning blue as his own flesh returned to a color he had not had in months. He was sick from overeating, and vomited up some flesh, but smiled as he burped, tasting the four men on the ground. As he calmed down and came to his senses, he decided he couldn't leave them like this. One at a time, he dragged them to an ancient dumpster and dropped them in. When the four of them were piled up on top of each other, he ran to the nearest car and pushed it down the street to the dumpster. The tires wouldn't roll, but Adam was so strong from his meal, it didn't stop him. When he had the car against the dumpster, he ripped off the gas cap and shoved a piece of one the men's shirts into the open gasoline port. He hopped up into the dumpster and fished through the men's jeans until he found a lighter and hopped back out. The shirt was now wet with gasoline, and when Adam lit it, it went up quickly. Adam was sprinting down the street when the car exploded, igniting the trash in the dumpster along with the four destroyed bodies that lay inside.

The run home was invigorating for the blood covered creature. It was after three in the morning by the time he had left the grisly scene, and the streets were mostly empty. He moved like a cheetah through the dark streets of New York, avoiding people by smelling, hearing or seeing them long before they knew he was near. When he got back to his own building, he scaled the side of the building, using his talons to climb straight up to his third floor apartment. He entered his unlocked window, took off his clothes and smelled them for a while before showering off the blood and pieces of human being that were stuck to him. When he was clean, he shoved his clothes into a bag and sent them down the garbage shoot of his apartment as he had done many times before. He went back to his bedroom, laid down on the fake fur coat which was on his bed, and curled up like a dog that had eaten too much. He closed his eyes, enjoyed the warmth and taste that lingered in his mouth, and dreamed of shredding the four men over and over.

Eighteen

Special Task Force
Friday Morning – 6th Precinct

The officers from both precincts sat drinking coffee around a long conference table that was covered with folders, some dating back as far as the sixties. They worked quietly until the person they were waiting for entered the room. Heather walked in with a large folder under her arm, said a quick good morning, and then walked to a whiteboard and grabbed an erasable marker.

She was writing quickly, in large block print, making columns with data in each row. She copied the information from her notes and worked in silence, the men sipping coffee and watching her until she was finished. When she had filled the board with information she turned around, looking fairly stressed out.

"Gentlemen, you are looking at almost two hundred files from all over the city. I have kept the investigation to within Manhattan for now, although who knows where this will end up. After working with every precinct in the city, and going through the notes you have made thus far, I am beginning to see the picture of something so bizarre I don't even know where to start. I have pulled some evidence from old files and sent them back to the labs for testing using current technologies. Most of these are dead-end files or missing person cases that went unsolved. Here's where we are…" She turned to the board and showed the columns, rattling off the information she had cross referenced over the past few days. "Every year, almost 900,000 people are reported as missing in this country. The vast majority of these are found relatively quickly. Here in the city, we had over 5,000 reports, of which approximately 4,700 were found. Of the three hundred missing that didn't turn up quickly with happy endings, about half ended up being homicides and a couple of suicides. That leaves about a hundred open missing persons cases. There were about 500 homicides last year, but most of these were solved and the killer was someone the victim knew—either a lover, an acquaintance, a drug or gang related death—stuff like that. Our crime statistics only go back to the sixties, but the number of unsolved murder cases and missing persons cases fluctuates from today's lows around 500 to the highs over 2200 back in the late nineties."

She took a breathe and looked around to make sure everyone was following her.

"Okay—so of the year's *combined* homicides and missing persons cases, we average about two hundred that go unsolved. If our killer wanted to have a new victim every week or two for the last fifty years, he could have theoretically done it. I mean, if he wanted to maintain his diet."

Everyone cringed but no one said anything.

"Are you people *listening* to me? I said *maintain his diet*! I have looked at over a hundred Jane or John Doe cases and unsolved homicides that fit a pattern of a killer that *potentially* eats parts of his victims."

Roy was seeing the skulls in the furnace in his head. "Excuse me, but how do you *potentially* partially eat someone?"

"*Thank you!* I am glad *someone* is listening to me," she said. "I say *potentially*, because *none* of the reports *say it* in so many words. No coroner's report, no crime scene report—no one will come out and say that the killer is drinking blood or eating chunks of his victims, but if you read carefully and go back far enough, you can see the same thing over and over again. There are a hundred crime scenes without substantial quantities of blood, even though the victims were brutally murdered. There are cases with victims missing organs, for God's sake, and no one thought *that* was significant? There are cases of body parts found in the city that were dead ends. I went back to the archives and even some newspaper stories back in the 1940's. Now—I'm not saying for sure that some old guy is running around eating people in New York…but I am saying that if there *was* one, it sure as hell is *possible*."

"Okay, so it's possible. I think we all believed it was possible after what we've been seeing so far. How does any of this help us catch this sick fuck?" asked Roy.

"What we have so far doesn't help us get *ahead* of him. We still can't develop patterns or find some type of MO. What we *can* do, is tell the chief that this is connected and open up a wider investigation. If this killer has in fact been at this for so long, I'm sure he has gotten quite good at covering his tracks. We are going to need more help. We can't get ahead of him yet, but maybe we can at least try and catch up to him."

"Is there any commonality with locations at *all*?" asked Captain Rosetto. "I mean, can we narrow it down even a *little* bit?"

"No. I have cases like this in all five boroughs, even though I am only working Manhattan right now. I have calls out to the State Police and FBI crime labs. The Feds are supposed to be calling me back today or tomorrow. Believe it or not, they are actually aware of some of what I was tippy-toeing around. I mean, I didn't use words like werewolf or vampire or Dahmer or anything, but they knew what I was getting at. They actually have a guy that specializes in this shit. I can't wait to talk to him. Anyway—what have *you* guys found?"

Tim looked at Pat. "You want to start?"

Pat cleared his throat. "Okay—this is what I have so far, and everyone keep your wiseass comments to yourself. I would never say any of this outside this room because I know I'd be sent on mandatory visits to the shrink. The skulls in the warehouse were obviously three different people. But DNA testing on other bone samples came up with a total of seven victims. One of the victims does match a missing person from last year. A woman named Rosa Santos with several priors for solicitation went missing last February. There was DNA on file, taken from her apartment, in case a body was ever recovered. We pushed the bones to the top of the pile over at the lab and *she* came back. Twenty-three years old, lived on forty-sixth and sixth, last seen near Central Park by her 'friend' who we know was her pimp. Homicide looked at him for her murder, but never could put anything together."

Heather crossed her arms. "What about the other six in there with her?"

"I should hear something any day. But it was Dr. Valesi's comments about the skulls that have me at a loss. He said he ran every canine impression in his library, and even a Bull Mastiff doesn't have fangs long enough to do what this guy did. A mastiff is a big fucking dog, people."

"So what does he think it was?" asked Tim Rosetto.

"He says something between a lion and a saber-toothed tiger. No shit. That's what he said."

"That's *great*, man. It shouldn't be too hard to find a prehistoric cat running around New York. I mean, even in *this* city, somebody would probably notice a saber toothed fucking tiger," said one of the men sarcastically. "What the fuck are we supposed to do with *that*?"

"I have no idea what you're supposed to do with it. I'm just telling you what the doc told me. It is not anything that fits anything he ever came across before. He sent bite reconstructions to the FBI office. Probably to the same guy that Heather is waiting on," said Pat. "Doc Valesi also gave me the name of another guy who now teaches over at NYU. I paid the guy a visit and asked him about the bite reconstruction model that Valesi made. The guy is an anthropology professor." He looked around apologetically. "I know—it sounds ridiculous. I'm just going where the doc pointed me. This professor kept me in his office for two hours looking at old books that showed pictures I am not even going to discuss here."

"Oh, come on, man. If he told you anything that can help us, don't hold out on us," said Tim.

"It's ridiculous," said Pat quietly.

The men all started talking at once, now curious about what the mystery professor was talking about.

Pat raised his hands. "Fine. You want to know what I listened to for two hours? Urban legends. Two hours of werewolves and vampires and myths that have been handed down for a thousand years in all parts of the world. I didn't know whether I should laugh or cry. You can't even imagine the shit he made me sit through. But…"

Everyone waited. Finally, Heather asked him. "But *what?*"

"One of the stupid fucking stories had a picture in it. Some medieval book about superstitious bullshit. The picture in the book matched the bite reconstruction model pretty closely. It was just a legend. It just… it just looked like the fucking model." He was staring at the table, obviously embarrassed and maybe a little shaken up.

"And what did it look like?" asked Lt. Alexander.

"You don't even want to know," replied Pat quietly.

"Of *course* I want to know. We *all* want to know! What did it look like?"

"Some kind of fucking *vampire*. The story was about how some undead thing killed an entire village over the course of a year in some remote part of Eastern Europe. It's old legend. It's fictional bullshit. It just so happens that it fits."

Nineteen

Friday, preparing for Date Night

Adam was actually nervous about "going out on a date". You'd think that when a man reached two hundred or so years old, he'd be smoother about such things, but Adam hadn't been on anything resembling a date since he ate Renee back in 1861. He was determined not to eat and drink Sara if it was at all possible. At least, not on the first date.

Adam looked at himself in the mirror. His color was still excellent, his eyes nice and blue, and his skin must be warm to the touch since he was still able to use his breathe to fog the mirror in his bathroom. Most of the time, when his heart wasn't beating and breathe wasn't coming out of his lungs, his skin was cold and white, and his eyes were silvery. That was when he knew it was time to feed. While he could eat every day and always keep himself more "human", the complications that came with so much murder would eventually cause him problems, and he knew it.

As Adam's thoughts drifted back to feeding and times past, he remembered more than one situation that had gotten him caught, and if he *could* be killed, those were the times when he must have been closest to his own demise.

While Adam was never sure why the thing in the woods died the day it infected him, he *did* know that the creature, his creator, had eaten heavily before the attack. It must have been feeling quite "alive" as Adam did after he ate. Perhaps it was when he was alive and his heart beat with the blood of other mortals that he was most vulnerable? It was one of many theories, but he still wasn't sure. Adam had been "wounded" many times, but only "hurt" once. While feeding, it was common for his prey to fight back. He actually enjoyed *that*, as it made the victims pump the endorphins and adrenaline that he coveted so. During those times over the decades, he had been shot, stabbed, slashed, pummeled with clubs, bats and pipes, even burned. What he noticed was that as soon as he fed, the wounds disappeared very quickly, and his appearance was never permanently scarred. Except that one time. His thoughts traveled back a hundred plus years.

Back in 1864, while traveling with the Union Army near Cedar Creek, he was enjoying the "spoils of war" and eating several wounded men in some woods the way he usually snuck his meals. Adam, by that time already using the name Adam Priest instead of Olmer Bartha, would stay with a unit as it fought, disappearing occasionally to feed, and then often times join up somewhere else. He was never questioned about disappearing, as he would do it during heavy fighting, and missing and dead soldiers were too numerous to keep track of. When he reappeared before battles, he would be shoved into line with the others, and no one ever took notice of the undead soldier living among so many other "walking dead". On one particular day, after heavy fighting gave way to sunset, both sides fell back into protected positions to camp for the evening. Adam snuck off, feeling a strong desire to feed after seeing so much blood all day.

Adam moved quietly into some woods, where some wounded union soldiers were resting in a glade, trying to tend to each other's wounds as they awaited a corpsman. Adam's lust was beyond control, after smelling fear, sweat, testosterone, adrenaline and endorphins in such quantities they were intoxicating. At one point, a cannonball had removed the head of a man nearby and sprayed Adam and several others with brains and blood as they pressed forward. Only Adam licked his lips and snarled, wanting to suck out the warm liquids from the man's open neck, while the others fought back the urge to vomit or just start running away. Unbeknownst to Adam, it was his own growling and howling that inspired the men around him to push forward and attack amidst the shelling and musket fire that rained down on them.

When Adam quietly entered the glade, he found a man on the ground, braced against a tree and holding his stomach where he had been "gut shot." Adam glanced around, and seeing no one nearby, leaned over to comfort the injured man. He bit through the man's throat and drank heavily, crazed by the day's events. When he had sucked the man dry, he moved through the woods silently, finding another man not far from the first. He drank that man dry as well, overfeeding to the point of nausea, but was now in full blood lust with claws and teeth showing in the dim light. His eyes were darkened to blue in the dim woods, and his face was covered in blood and entrails. He moved to the next victim, who was also leaning against a tree, his left leg wrapped with a tourniquet above a shattered lower leg. Adam's heart was pounding with the blood of the first two victims, but he could smell this man's blood as it bubbled from under the make-shift bandages. He moved slowly towards him, eyeing the pulpy lower leg as he licked his lips between blood soaked fangs.

The man on the ground, a Union major, eyed the thing as it came towards him. He was at first quite sure he was seeing the Devil himself, coming to take him to Hell, but then realized the Devil was wearing a Union infantry uniform. The thing was moving towards slowly and quietly, its mouth covered in blood and bits of flesh. It was eyeing his pulverized leg and salivating on itself. As it moved in to feed, the major raised the pistol that was in his hand and aimed it square at the thing's chest. He fired the large Colt and watched the thing spin wildly before hitting the ground. The creature looked down at its own chest and saw blood pumping from the large hole. The major saw a look of surprise on the thing's face, and then pain. It howled loudly, filling the woods with a sound that made every survivor's hair stand up.

The major raised his weak arm a second time, using every ounce of strength to pull the hammer back for a second shot, but the creature pounced. The animal, wounded and screaming, leapt onto the prone man and used clawed hands to tear the man's head from his body. The major's head came off with a pop noise, and Adam shoved his face into the geyser of blood, slurping and sucking up the arterial spray like a man at a water fountain. He fed until he was vomiting the blood back up, and then slowly moved through the now-dark woods to drop and rest. As he lay on the ground, he became aware of a pain in his chest and back. The large caliber bullet had passed through him, something that had happened many times before, but this time—it *hurt*.

Adam rolled onto his back, his claws and fangs slowly receding.

He smelled blood coming from his wound. It was the mixture from the three other men. He listened to his own heart pumping with their blood, but instead of feeling strong from the feeding, he felt weak. He smiled. It felt so human. Adam spent the night listening to men cry all around him from the dark woods and battlefield beyond the trees. It reminded him of Jena. He could hear hearts stop beating. He could feel death around him—smell it even. It was delicious. He passed out, weak and in pain, but feeling total ecstasy.

When he awoke at first light, there were orderlies in the woods picking up wounded men in litters and carrying them to the field hospital. He sat up and felt strange. He slid a finger into the hole in his chest, and was surprised to find that it hadn't yet completely healed. The hole was clammy and raw, but did not bleed. He pondered that a moment. Perhaps when he was full of blood and his heart beat like a living human, he was vulnerable? Would the wound heal? He was playing with the hole when two corpsmen approached him.

"Hey, corporal. You better come with us. The doc should give that a look-see. You feeling okay enough to stand?"

Adam stood, and felt almost normal. "I'm fine," he said quietly. "See to the others."

They looked at his uniform, covered in blood, and at his pale face with silvery eyes that looked like those of a dead man. "I think you ought to come with us, friend. You been shot," said the young corpsman, walking towards him.

Adam looked at him and snarled, with anger creeping into his voice. "I said I'm fine. Move on."

The corpsman shrugged and walked away. It wasn't so uncommon for soldiers to avoid the surgeons, especially if they had limb wounds and didn't want to face the saw. "Suit yourself," said the boy, disappearing into the woods to find another bloody mess of a human.

Adam left the woods, rejoined an infantry unit, and fought for another two days before he was able to feed again. After that second heavy feeding, he was back to his old self, but noticed that the bullet hole did leave a scar in his chest. His one and only.

Adam opened his eyes and realized he was still in his bathroom. It was still 2011, and he still needed to dress for his date. He smiled and looked at the ancient scar on his chest. He pushed the questions out of his head and picked some clothes from his closet.

As Adam dressed, he pondered the evening ahead of him. Eating and drinking anything other than living blood and occasional small bits of tissue was out of the question. He had tasted wine before, and while he found the smells to be very pleasant, actually drinking the liquid would make him feel extremely ill. How would he "take the girl out" without eating himself? This was a logistical problem that would require creativity. He was intelligent—he'd think of something...

Twenty

The Date

Adam and Sara had decided to meet in Midtown. He had purchased tickets for a Broadway Show, an impressive first date. Money was no object to a creature that had been murdering humans for so many decades. Once, when he was going through a box of old money, he came upon a large stash of very old gold coins. He realized they were worth more than spending money, and a coin dealer in New York had paid him almost forty thousand dollars for coins he thought might be worth a couple of thousand. He had similar experiences with art and a few other objects of antiquity he had acquired over the decades. He could afford to "be a sport".

Adam was standing on the corner of Times Square and Forty-Eighth Street awaiting Sara when her taxi pulled up. He paid the driver before she could do it herself, and although she tried to fight him for the fare, he could see she was already impressed with his chivalry. He smiled at her when she got out of the yellow cab, and she kissed his warm cheek a cheery "hello."

It was only six o'clock, and their show wouldn't start until eight. They had planned to have a quick bite before the show, although not the type of bite Adam would have preferred on most such encounters.

"So nice to see you again, Adam," she said with a smile as she linked her arm through his. "You still haven't told me what show we are going to see…"

He looked at her and watched her smile with great satisfaction. He had somehow put that smile there himself, and found that quite interesting after so many years of causing reactions that were so different.

"Perhaps you like surprises," he said mysteriously, his own blue eyes sparkling back at hers.

"*Ooooh*," she cooed, feigning great intrigue.

"Hungry?" he asked. He could smell her perfume and hear her blood rushing hard in her throat. Her heart was beating slightly faster than normal. She was excited to see him, and it made him smile even broader.

"I could force myself, I'm sure," she said looking at his smile.

He thought about how he would like to force his teeth through her thigh, but resisted.

"Do you like sushi?" he asked.

"Oh my God—are you *kidding*? It's my favorite food," she said. She cocked her head and eyed him suspiciously. "Seriously—did I mention that to you already, or do you like it, too?"

"I love it. I know just the place," he said. Prior to picking her up, he had thought long and hard about how he would pull this "date thing" off. He recalled having eaten fish a few times in his life when he was desperate to feed. They were cold blooded creatures and their blood was nothing at all like a mammal's, but their oils and flesh were digestible so long as it was very fresh and uncooked. It had been decades since he had touched a fish, and he had stopped at a sushi bar to try it again before he picked her up. He found it barely tolerable, but it was all he could think of that would pass in front of Sara.

They walked, arm in arm, down a few streets until they came to a sushi bar that had a small line outside.

"Oh my God," Sara said quietly. "You really *are* trying to impress me," she said as she nudged his ribs. "But unless you called weeks ago, we'll never get in. Kazu is the best sushi place in the city. Well, from what I'm told anyway."

"So you haven't been here before?" he asked. The average price per person was easily three hundred dollars. He was guessing "no".

"Um, no. I've heard lots a great things about Kazu, the sushi chef, but I've never actually been here."

"I am told he is one of the best in New York. Perhaps anywhere," he said, looking deeply into her blue-green eyes. He kept walking, and ignored the line as he entered the tiny restaurant. He had stopped by earlier, handed the hostess four hundred dollars, and said he and a date would need a table for two in the back corner. She had immediately put him on the guest list. The young Japanese girl spotted him as he re-entered, this time with his date, and bowed, then showed him to his table in the back of the long narrow restaurant.

Sara was amazed. The floors were tile and wood, and every table and chair was handmade from fine woods. Fresh flowers and a waterfall decorated the dimly lit restaurant. Several movie stars and New York politicians sat in small booths or at the long sushi bar in front of Kazu and his assistants. The hostess seated them in the rear booth, across from a waterfall built into the marble wall across from them. It was quiet and absolutely beautiful.

"I can't believe you are taking me here!" she whispered to him from across the booth. "We could skip the show and stay here all night!" she said with a huge grin. She realized what she said may have not had the intended complimentary result, and added, "But of course I am excited to see the show—I just meant, this place is amazing!"

He smiled, and could feel her excitement. She was an interesting woman. So alive. It was contagious, really. He inhaled her from across the table. While the humans would have smelled sandalwood and flowers, he could smell fish oil, and did not particularly like it. The hint of sandalwood reminded him of the woods in Jena, but the fish odors ruined the memory. He concentrated on Sara's perfume, which he found delightful. It mixed with her skin chemistry and made the hair on his arms tingle. He slid his tongue across his teeth and tasted her scent, his eyes fluttering. She watched him, curiously.

"Starving?" she asked him.

He smiled, wondering how delicious she would taste, but fought hard against those images. He was still quite full from the previous feeding, and those strong men had his heart pumping hard and his own flesh warm to the touch. "Starving? No. But I can always eat something delicious," he said quietly, trying not to stare at the blood pumping in her carotid artery.

Sarah blushed.

The waitress approached them and bowed, and Adam shocked Sara by speaking a few words in Japanese to her. They conversed quickly; she bowed again, and walked away.

"You speak Japanese?" she asked, quite impressed.

"Only a bit. I have traveled quite extensively, and always found languages to be very interesting. I speak a little bit of several. You?"

"I'm pretty good with English," she joked. "Actually, I am trying to learn a little Spanish, but don't put enough time into it."

Adam rattled off some Spanish to her, and it was Castilian Spanish from Spain, not Mexico. His accent was perfect, and it sounded beautiful to Sara. "Wow, that is so different from what I hear around here," she replied softly.

"I learned my Spanish in Spain," he explained. "Like British English versus American English. A bit more proper perhaps?"

"It's beautiful. You are a very interesting man, Adam Priest," she said with a smile. "What other languages do you speak?" She leaned closer to him as she spoke across the table, and her body language wasn't lost on Adam.

"Well, I am not fluent in most of these, but I speak English, Spanish, French, German, Portuguese, Old Prussian, and a bit of Japanese, Mandarin, and Russian."

Sara sat back, amazed. "That is so cool. I wish I could speak languages like that. I am very impressed, Mr. Priest," she said with a smile. "Have you traveled a lot, then?"

"Quite a bit, actually. What about you? I know nothing about you…"

"There isn't nearly as much to tell about me. I want to hear all about you!" she said, and this time took his hand in hers. "You, sir, are the most interesting man I have met, maybe, ever."

Adam smiled at her. He really did feel something for this woman. Perhaps it was because she was so obviously drawn to him, or perhaps because she was in fact a beautiful woman with some intelligence. Or maybe it was simply that he really wanted to tear her chest open and eat her heart while it still beat. In any event, he enjoyed being around her and feeling her energy.

"Enough about me..." he said, as the waitress arrived carrying a large carafe of hot sake and two small cups. She placed them on the table, and picked it up to pour, but Adam spoke to her in Japanese, and she bowed and left. "Allow me," he said, and he picked up the carafe and poured one for her. He then lifted the carafe to his own cup, and faked filling it. The tiny ceramic cups were opaque, and she could not tell that his was empty. "Compai," he toasted in Japanese, and touched her cup. She toasted him back and drank her sake, and he quickly refilled hers while again faking his own. He knew that when humans were pleasantly plied with alcohol, their guard was down and they were much less observant. The more she drank, the less she would notice about his eating habits.

They chatted for a while, enjoying each other's company, and then the waitress returned with a large tray of beautifully arranged fish. Tuna, yellowtail, salmon and flying fish roe, Japanese Snapper, and several other specialties were arranged "just so" by the master chef. Adam and the waitress spoke Japanese for a moment, and she smiled and thanked him before she left.

Sara poured soy sauce into her tiny soy plate and mixed wasabi into it with her chopsticks. She picked up some wasabi and went to place it in Adam's dish, and he cringed.

"No! Thank you," he said as calmly as he could. The smell of the hot horseradish was repugnant, and the smell of the salty soy sauce was overpowering. He felt slightly ill, but faked a smile. "I prefer the delicate nature of the fish without any sauce. I think I am a bit allergic to the wasabi," he added.

She smiled and shrugged, and picked up a piece of sushi. "This looks amazing. Thank you so much for bringing me here, Adam."

Adam reached for a piece of tuna sashimi, and smiled as he placed it in his mouth, the first dead meal he had eaten in decades, other than trying it earlier in the day to experiment with it. As the fatty tuna dissolved on his tongue, he closed his eyes and pretended it was Sara's liver, then reopened his eyes to watch her eat her own fish with great enjoyment. He continued to push the sake on her until she was quite pleasantly "buzzed".

Dinner was a smash success, and by the time they left, she was very physical with her date, her arm around him as they walked down the street. She pulled him close on the street and kissed him on the mouth, thanking him for the best sushi dinner she had ever experienced in her life. He enjoyed the kiss, fighting back the urge to devour her, and instead smelled her hair and perfume and skin and wondering what she would look like naked. Such a human thought.

They walked together to the theatre, where they sat orchestra center to see "Phantom", an appropriate show for such an odd couple.

Twenty-One

Taskforce

It was Friday night, and the taskforce had ordered in a bunch of pizzas and sodas and decided to stay late and brainstorm together over piles of new information they had received from the Feds, the State Police, and NYPD precincts all over the city. Tim picked up the folder that Pat Ammiano had given him from the anthropology professor and called over to Roy.

"Hey—Roy, you just got volunteered. Come on, we're taking a ride uptown."

"Whatcha got?" he asked.

Tim made a face. "If I tell you, you won't come." He replied, and got up to leave.

"It ain't another fucked up crime scene, is it?" he asked.

"Nope. Just a fucked up person. Come on."

The two of them rode the elevator downstairs and took Captain Rosetto's unmarked car uptown into a part of town that was almost completely black, filled with immigrants from all over the Caribbean. Haitians, Jamaicans, Dominicans, you name the island—it was represented in the neighborhood. They pulled up in front of a large church, painted in bright colors reminiscent of their Caribbean homes. The two men got out and walked up the stairs to the old church. It was late on a Friday, and the church was almost empty, except for a few priests in bright robes. Candles burned all over the church, and small statues of saints unknown to white churchgoers had many candles lit in their honor. They walked down the aisle and approached one of the priests.

"Excuse me, father," said Tim quietly. "I am looking for Father Eduardo."

The man looked at Tim, eyeing the large white man suspiciously before speaking.

"You are police?" he asked.

"Yes," he said, and flipped his badge. "I came for some help. I was told Father Eduardo might be able to answer some questions pertaining to a case we are working on."

"Conversations between priests and their parishioners are confidential..." he began.

"No, no—it's nothing like that. I just need some help. I think he can shed a little light on something, that's all."

The priest stood for a moment, sizing them both up, and then told them to follow him to a small room in the back of the altar. They entered the office and found a very old, very bizarre looking dwarf sitting on a leather couch reading from an ancient leather book. Father

Eduardo was under four feet tall, with white hair and a white beard that extended to his stomach. Seeing him wearing a bright African styled hat and robe, they felt like they had stepped into another country. The man slid off the couch and hopped to his feet. Even with his black, red and green leather cap, he was still only belt-high to the officers. Roy and Tim tried not to react to the man's size or costume.

"Hello Father Eduardo," said Tim. "My name is Tim Rosetto. I'm a Detective Captain from the Sixth precinct and this is Sergeant Roy Ruiz from Midtown North. We're working on something out of the ordinary, and we've been pointed in your direction. I was wondering if you might give us a little of your time?"

Father Eduardo opened his arms dramatically, and although he was tiny in stature, he had a great presence. "I am always ready to help 'dose who seek my council," he said with a very heavy accent that was hard to place. He sounded Creole, maybe, his consonants hard on his tongue, and his voice deep and booming for such a tiny person. "Come and be seated wit' me" he said, and he climbed back up on the coach. Tim and Roy found seats opposite him, and the other priest walked out and closed the door behind him.

Father Eduardo folded his pudgy fingers in his lap, his robe a rich red, embroidered with gold thread and multicolored beads. "And tell me now, what brings you to me?"

Tim cleared his throat. He had rehearsed this a dozen times in his head, and no matter how he said it, he sounded insane. He would not make eye contact with Roy for fear of being humiliated. "Well, Father Eduardo, this is going to sound very strange, I'm afraid. But we've come across something that is very difficult to explain. We are open to looking at anything that can give us some clues as to what it is we are looking for, and I was pointed to you by a professor of anthropology named Dr. Cook."

The old man smiled, showing a few gaps and gold teeth. "Ahh, yes. Doctor Cook is a good man. He and I have chatted many times over the years. He has an open mind and understands more about the cultures of the Islanders and Africans than most white men, no offense."

"None taken, Father. I'll be blunt. We are working a murder investigation, and I need your word on total secrecy, okay?"

He nodded and said, "Of course," quietly.

"We have been investigating a string of murders that appear to be connected, and appear to involve some sort of ritualized, um...well... cannibalism."

Father Eduardo did not react with any shock. "Continue..." he said.

"Well, we are trying to put together some facts and common threads on many missing person cases and some bizarre homicides. The problem is, the attacker may, and I stress the word 'may', have been at this for a very long time. And the problem is, the murder weapon, well..." Tim searched for the words carefully and looked straight ahead, avoiding Roy's face. "The murder weapon may be the killer's teeth or maybe something he carries that looks like a claw. Honestly—it's so bizarre, we are stuck. The professor had some very troubling legends about monsters and such that he was eager to share with us—urban legends and the like, but one of the things he showed us fit a bite model that our lab guys put together. According to Dr. Cook, we are supposed to show it to you."

The old man exhaled slowly. He looked deeply troubled. "So you t'ink you are tracking a monster now here in da' city?"

"No, no, no...I'm not saying that! I'm just saying that Dr. Cook said you might have some explanation for what we have been seeing. The killer has been, um, well, drinking blood and eating parts of his victims in some type of ritual. Any of this mean anything to you?"

The dwarf slid down off the couch and walked across the room to a book shelf, where he pulled an old leather bound book almost as large as he was tall. "Mean anyt'ing to me?" He laughed, a deep booming laugh. "You t'ink dat monsters don't live in 'dis city because you an educated man. But 'dis country two hundred years old. The legends of 'dis country are borrowed from other countries that are *thousands* of years old. You t'ink monster stories are only to scare little children? You t'ink if it can't be explained it can't be real?" The priest placed the large book on his desk and stood on a chair to open the cover. "Let me see your bite model," he said, sounding gravely serious.

Tim reached into his overcoat and pulled a brown paper bag. "This is a lab reconstruction based on some bite marks we found on victims. It matches several victims. We have no idea what it is, but it is consistent, and something out there has teeth, or uses a weapon that looks like teeth, that matches this." Tim pulled out a set of teeth that could have been from a Hollywood movie set. Huge fangs protruded from the top upper and lower mandibles.

Father Eduardo made a face and crossed his arms, pacing back and forth. He finally spoke, after several moments of deep concentration.

"You are Catholics?" he asked the men, who both said yes. "So you both believe in good and evil and Heaven and Hell?" They both sort of shrugged, uneasy in their own religious beliefs in front of this man that looked more witch doctor than priest. The priest grunted. "Let me tell you some t'ings. You ever wonder why the poor black communities attend churches like 'dis one? You ever wonder why the African religions have so many evil spirit stories rooted in their religions? "Der are 'tings that can't be explained in the world, my friends. You live in a city where the last wild bear lived here a hundred years ago. People here t'ink a big dog or a rat is scary. Well in villages in Africa, wild animals come in at night and carry off people for food. And in the islands and the villages of Africa, where the people are more in tune with wild nature, they believe in t'ings you would never accept."

The priest opened the book and started going through pages, looking at the bite model every now and again.

"White Americans have no problem believing dinosaurs lived millions of years ago. The museums are filled with giant monsters that would eat you in a second, and everyone takes 'dis as *fact*. Why is it 'dat you are so selective in what monsters you believe and which you deny?" He pulled open a page and showed a huge monster-like man, with giant fangs, standing over several dead bodies. There was blood drawn everywhere in the picture, and the bodies were torn open at the necks, thighs, chest and arms. "You see 'dis picture? You see 'dem teeth? You see 'dem victims? It look familiar to you?"

It was just an old picture from an old book—total mythology from another place and time, but both Roy and Tim felt their hair stand up. The creature in the book had attacked the victims at their arteries the same way the victims in New York City had been attacked. Roy felt physically ill as he flashed back to "Goth Girl".

"Jesus Christ," said Tim quietly.

"Yes. "Dat's right. You better pray to Jesus Christ and to all of the Saints and God Almighty Hisself 'dat 'dis ting not walking the streets of your city. It is the *undead*. This creature been in Africa and Europe for a thousand years. Why you 'tink Dracula movies so popular? Why you 'tink people like horror movies? It's because the notions tickle survival skills and memories deep in the brain of creatures and predators we no longer have to deal with, but are in our collective conscious." He hopped off the chair and walked around the small office, arms waving as he spoke, now very animated.

"Why you 'tink people afraid of the de' dark? It's because fear keep you *alive*! It's because there were t'ings that fed in the dark for a few thousand years, and those humans that stayed awake or on guard lived. And 'dose that slept heavy were eaten. Go on—say it's crazy superstitious nonsense."

Tim finally looked at Roy, and Roy looked white as a sheet. Tim cleared his throat, his mouth now very dry. "Look, Father...I'm a detective. I deal in facts and evidence. I try and keep an open mind, and I admit I have seen some crazy stuff in this city. I'm not saying yes or no to anything you've shared with us, I'm just trying to collect as much information as I can, okay? What do the stories from your culture say about this thing?"

"It isn't just *my* culture, policeman. Eastern Europe and Russia was full of such demon stories. Look at pictures from frescos in Italy. Dante's Inferno—his idea of Hell. Always blood and violence in every human culture. The same 'tings have scared humans for as long as we have walked on 'dis Earth. And maybe the *dinosaurs* all died. But *these* t'ings...they still here. And now you gotta find 'dis one."

"And what do we do when we find it?" asked Roy, finally speaking out loud.

The man walked to Roy with fire in his eyes. He leaned close to Roy's face and hissed, "Den you *kill* it!"

"How?" asked Roy, his face an expression of stark fear.

The old man nodded and walked around the office for a moment. "Dat is the harder task for you. The books and legends tell of these monsters. And I have seen pictures of the monsters heads up on pikes. So I know dey can be killed. I just don't know how." He played with his long white beard for a while, still walking in circles.

"How many people dis ting kill?"

"We don't know. We do have some evidence that suggests he may be sixty or seventy years old though. He might have killed a lot of people. We just don't know," said Tim quietly, still trying to digest what this man had suggested.

"Sixty or seventy is nothing. Dis creature might be a thousand years old. It is *undead*. It is *cursed*. It eats human blood and tissue to stay alive. Der are stories of whole villages being eaten over the course of month or years. It will just keep feeding until you kill it. Dis t'ing...it is strong. It is not afraid of anything. And it will be difficult to kill. I will pray for you," he said quietly.

Tim and Roy looked at each other. This was apparently the end of the scare session. They thanked Father Eduardo for his time, took their bite model, and walked back out to car in silence.

When they closed the car doors they looked at each other.

"He scare you?" asked Tim.

"Shitless," said Roy quietly.

"Me, too."

Twenty-Two

Adam & Sara

They walked out of the show with Sara holding on to Adam's arm very tightly. She was sniffling and resting her head on his shoulder as they walked out into the street. They hadn't walked far when she stopped and pulled him to her.

"Adam, I don't know what to say. This has been one of the best nights I have had in a long, long time. The show was beautiful. I bawled my eyes out. The music, the acting, it was amazing. And dinner? And you…" she leaned in and gave him a hug, then looked up waiting for a kiss.

Adam looked down at her and actually felt something human. He wasn't sure what it was. His heart was still beating with the blood of four men he had recently eaten, and he wasn't hungry for Sara's blood, but he felt something for her—a need to be close to her, perhaps. Decades ignoring anything that felt like loneliness seemed to creep into his being. He leaned down and kissed her mouth, hoping his own mouth didn't taste like death or blood. Sara's own breath tasted of sake, and most likely, that was all she tasted as she kissed him deeply. Adam tried to recall kissing a human like this. Renee perhaps? It was so long ago, he couldn't be sure. But he did enjoy her taste and her smell. And something else—her company.

"Want to take me home now?" she asked quietly as they broke their kiss.

He smiled and wondered about that. Was their date over, or did she want to have sex with him? Humans did love to copulate, he knew well. But if he did go back with her, would he be able to keep the animal inside all night long? He enjoyed this woman. He would have to be very careful. He really didn't want to eat her.

She laughed out loud. "I'm sorry—I didn't mean it the way I said it. I just mean, it's getting late. If you want, you can take a ride back to my place and we can have a glass of wine or something, that's all. You've been such a great host all night, it's my turn to buy you a drink."

Adam smiled. "Sure," he said. "I'd love to see where you live."

They grabbed a cab and drove across town a bit and she stopped the cabbie in front of a beautiful brownstone building. It was an old building, but kept up very well. It was very "old world" and charming. It reminded Adam a bit of Europe. He flashed to Renee, naked, covered in blood after days of having sex with her and feeling almost human. He sighed and kept the talons in.

They got out and Sara opened the front door for him, and then led him down a small hallway to her apartment on the ground floor. She opened the door to a spacious home, with hardwood floors covered by Persian rugs, and pretty furniture that seemed very feminine. He admired her collection of art and photos that adorned her walls. It was definitely the apartment of a human woman.

"Come in," she said. "What do you think?" She entered quickly and headed to a wine rack. "Do you prefer red or white?" she asked. He contemplated that. He much preferred the smell of red wine, its subtleties very interesting, like the subtleties of blood. But knowing he couldn't drink it, and knowing he would be pouring it around her apartment, he requested white.

"I would have pegged you for a red man, myself," she said with a smile. "But I have some nice white. You like French?"

He thought of Renee again, her throat exploded hot blood into his mouth. "Oh yes, French is wonderful," he said.

He watched her move in her kitchen quickly and efficiently, grabbing glasses and popping the cork as he wandered about, admiring her photos. He realized she had signed them.

"You are the photographer?" he asked.

"Yes," she replied as she returned with two glasses of white. "They aren't great, but I think I'm getting better. That's my favorite," she said, pointing to a dancer on the street done in black and white.

"Ah, like your friend Gellman?" he asked.

She cocked her head and looked at it. "That's so funny," she said. "I never really thought about that. I've looked at that picture a million times and didn't get it. You're so right. The body position is like hers, huh?"

Adam walked over to Sara and put his hands around her waist. "Yes, Gellman seemed to like the arched bodies, the strain in the muscles… very sensual, don't you think?"

Sara was still holding the glasses and she blushed. Adam kissed her neck, smelling her hair and skin and perfume and fighting to keep his fangs from sliding out. He wasn't hungry at all—there was no need to feed, but he did feel a hunger for this woman that made him smile. He could feel her heart beat slightly faster as he kissed her neck and even let his human teeth slide over her skin.

She giggled and her skin got goose bumps on her connected arm. "No marks!" she said jokingly. He smiled and pictured her throat ripped open.

"No marks," he said quietly, and took the glasses from her. She allowed him to take them from her, realizing his intentions, and not resisting.

"It's only our first date," she said quietly as she put her arms around his broad shoulders.

"The first of many, I hope," he said softly, and leaned in to kiss her. They kissed, more passionately as they went, and Adam was very aware of his date becoming lost in her passion as her heart increased its speed and her hormones began to pump into her bloodstream. He could feel it building inside her quickly, and had to fight so hard not to open her arteries. She would be so delicious, he was sure.

Adam picked her up and brought her to her large sofa, then placed her in the center of it. He knelt between her legs and pushed up her sweater dress slowly, feeling the leather of her tall boots and then the soft skin of her legs.

"Adam..." she whispered, trying to control her sexual urges that Adam could smell and practically taste. "It's our first date, I don't want to ruin it, okay?" she whispered.

He ignored her and slid her dress up slightly higher, then gently opened her legs wider, and kissed the inside of her thigh. He could feel the heat through her panties, smell her sex and hear the blood pumping harder through her veins. She whispered a soft, "Don't", which he ignored as he continued kissing up her thigh to her femoral artery. He was trying so hard to keep the fangs from sliding into feeding position. His claws were tingling in his fingertips, but he kept them inside. His mouth brushed over her silk panties, and he exhaled his warm living breath over her pubic mound, making her slide down closer to him as her legs spread wider. She was breathing heavier now, and he listened to her softly moaning as he teased her.

Adam began kissing her outside her panties, and then licked her crotch and let his hands slide over her soft warm thighs. She began groaning louder and he could feel her panties getting damp from the inside. She was so *alive*, he thought to himself—her senses so heightened in her sexually hungry state of arousal. Perhaps she could start to understand how he felt around blood, and he pulled her panties to one side as he slowly buried his warm, long tongue deep inside her. She grabbed his head and pressed against his mouth, moaning loudly as she orgasmed quickly, lost in her own bliss, forgetting her rules about first dates. Adam took his time, enjoying her smells and tastes and the pounding of her blood inside her heart and arteries. She climaxed several more times and finally screamed for him to stop. He leaned away from her and looked up at her, his face wet with her, but not covered in her blood.

"Oh my God, Adam" she said over and over. "Stand up!"

He stood and she fumbled with his belt and unsnapped his pants, pulling his slacks to the floor and quickly taking him inside her mouth. He smiled as he looked down at her. She was obviously trying very hard to please him, and *that* was something he hadn't felt in decades. It was as arousing as her mouth, and he felt the blood of the four men he had eaten pounding inside his sexual organ as it grew larger and harder. He was lost in thought when Sara snapped him back to the present and shouted, "I want you inside me," as she slid lower on the couch and ripped her panties off over the boots that were still on...

Twenty-Three

Sixth Precinct Taskforce – Saturday Morning

The group had reassembled Saturday morning at ten, and Captain Ammiano had even sprung for a box of good coffee and doughnuts. The officers helped themselves to coffee and doughnuts, Tim taking two to no one's surprise, and sat down around the large table. Heather entered the room with a professional looking gentleman in a suit. He had "FBI" written all over him.

"Good morning everyone. This is FBI Special Agent Doug Patmore. Agent Patmore works in a special service unit and has been assigned to help us with our case." She extended her hand to the Agent, who stepped forward and addressed the room. Doug Patmore was mid-forties, in excellent physical shape, and had a typical cop haircut—high and tight. His blonde hair and blue eyes made him look like a recruiting poster for the Feds.

"Good morning everyone. Doctor Connell is correct that I am in a special service unit, but I'm not sure whether I have been assigned to help you with your case, or use you to help me with mine. The cases you are following up on and investigating overlap a special project I have been working on for almost two years. My 'special service unit' works with Missing Persons, Unsolved Violent Crimes, Homicide, and Sexual Assaults. I am a 'unit of one'. My job is to is to find the overlaps in the cases from all of the units I have mentioned as they pertain to solving one particular case—the same one you are working on now."

"And that would be the cannibal-vampire-werewolf-monster creature that's approximately a thousand years old?" asked Tim with a mouthful of doughnut.

"You are further along in your investigation than I expected," he said, only half smiling.

Tim wiped his face and swallowed. "Seriously Agent Patmore..."

"You can call me Doug," he said.

"Okay, Doug. Seriously. Tell us what the fuck is going on. Yesterday, me and Roy here visited with Father Eduardo from some VooDoo church uptown who is completely convinced we are dealing with a monster that drinks human blood. We have a bite model for something that isn't human, but has appeared at our crime scenes, which are leaving a trail of half eaten bodies..."

"He's *eating* half of the bodies now?" asked Doug. The room went silent. "He used to only drink the blood and eat small pieces. Has he begun eating *more*?"

"Are you fucking *kidding* me?" asked one of the patrolman, putting down his doughnut.

The fed looked at him, and he wasn't smiling. Doug walked closer and pulled a chair, joining the group at the table. "I have been tracking an individual—at least I believe it is an individual—for twenty months. My unit originally had three agents in it, but homeland security issues have stretched manpower, and now my unit is just me. I have investigated almost two hundred and fifty missing persons and unsolved homicide cases, just like you have been doing, and I keep coming up with the same scenario. The killer, or possibly killers, are draining the victims of their blood, possibly even drinking it. The victims have been torn up pretty badly at almost every crime scene, and some of them were missing organs or had organs half eaten. Bone and wound marks indicate something that looks like animal fangs, or a human using something made to look that way. Some female victims, but not many, appear to have been sexually assaulted, but the sexual attacks seem secondary to the violent nature of the murders. Quite frankly, I think the attacker gets off from the killing so much he doesn't need to have sex with the victims. I have spent more hours than I care to admit working with FBI psychiatrists and analysts trying to build a profile on this guy. The opinions of our professionals vary enough to make all of them useless."

"Any of your professionals have a vampire-werewolf-cannibal theory?" asked Roy.

Doug paused. "Just me." The room remained silent.

The officers looked at each other for a moment. Doug cleared his throat. "Gentlemen, and lady, I have spent almost two years of my life following facts that are unbelievable. The lab techs I have worked with can't explain a lot of what we have found. The problem we face is not only the horrible nature of the crimes we have come across, but also the professional way in which they are carried out. This guy isn't a Charlie Manson type who leaves lots of gory mess for the papers to talk about.

We believe this has been going on for years, maybe decades, and this guy has yet to be even *remotely* in anyone's radar."

"We found fingerprints from a 1959 unsolved homicide at a crime scene last week in which the victim was sexually assaulted in some way, prior to being partially eaten and bleeding to death in a room with very little blood," said Heather quietly.

"And I have cases with evidence that suggest the same perpetrator going back even further, when fingerprinting was in its infancy," said Doug. "And I also have cases that cite specific patterns going back much, much further than that."

"Yeah, like maybe a thousand years or so, give or take?" asked Tim.

"Give or take," said Doug quietly.

Captain Ammiano had heard all he could take. "Does someone want to clue me in about what the *fuck* you are all talking about? How did we go from a possible multiple murder suspect to a thousand year old *vampire*? Are you people fucking *kidding* me?" Ammiano's face was a pleasant shade of purple.

Doug took a breath and began again. "Captain, with all due respect, the case that has been put together over the past two years defies convention. There are aspects of this case which are almost impossible to believe, but quite frankly, I am beyond caring about whether I believe it or not. I just want to catch up to this maniac so I can arrest him."

"So you did say *him*, not 'it'," said Tim.

Doug shrugged. "Have you looked at cases outside the city?" he asked. They all shook their heads no. "Well, I have. I've looked around the country, and I've looked around the world. If you think you feel self conscious asking other cops in the City about cases like this, try using Interpol to track 'vampire – cannibal killers'. I've had agents in other countries hang up on me. I've also had a few thank me for asking about these cases so they knew they weren't nuts. There are cases like this one all over the world folks. And they aren't anything new. And as far as Father Eduardo goes, I have spoken to him myself, although it was quite a while ago. I've also spoken to clergy from other parts of this country and around the world. I have even traveled to other countries to conduct face to face interviews. Quite frankly, I am surprised I haven't been taken off of this case and committed to a psych ward based on some of my own reports. We are dealing with some very strange circumstances."

"No shit," said Roy quietly.

Captain Ammiano lit a cigarette directly below the "no smoking" sign. His hands were trembling only slightly. "Okay, so let me get this straight. The FBI—the fucking FBI of my country—is officially investigating something they consider supernatural, or a monster or vampire or some shit. That is your official fucking case?" He was trying very hard to sound like he didn't believe any of it.

"Captain Ammiano, twenty months ago, I wouldn't have believed any of this, either. And honestly, this case is so bizarre; we can't go to the public with it. Most of our cases are solved with help from the public. But what are we supposed to ask in this case? 'If anyone has any information regarding a vampire, please call your local FBI office?' We have *more* than enough crazies calling in daily now. Sorry to say, we need to solve this one on our own, and I hope the people in this room are going to help me. This killer—human, animal, whatever it is, is currently residing in your city. I *am* pretty sure about *that*. This city has more strange cases that relate to my file than any other place on Earth, and unless you are fine with finding torn up corpses all over The Big Apple, I suggest everyone open their mind to possibilities that you couldn't imagine a week ago."

Heather folded her arms and made a face. "Agent Patmore, we had a similar discussion a week ago. About keeping an open mind, I mean. What we *do* need, is access to whatever information you have. Evidence, photos, leads, *everything.* Anything that helps this taskforce. We want to catch this animal. And human or not—he *is* an animal. I have been to a few crime scenes. This killer is unlike anything we've ever seen before."

"You have my full cooperation, just like I hope I have yours. And yes, Captain Ammiano, I understand your skepticism, and it's okay. Just keep an open mind and help me catch this guy before he kills again."

Tim's cell phone rang and he looked at the number and excused himself. He walked to a corner of the room and spoke quietly for a while, then came back to the table with a grave face.

"Well, one of my buds uptown just called me to tell me they have four stiffs in the morgue. All gangbangers with priors, so it's no huge surprise that they'd be victims of violent crime. Except that the coroner, who'd been put on notice by us to look for weird shit like this, just called to tell me that the victims had been killed with extreme violence, some had apparent bite marks, and had been torn up as if by wild animals—prior to being set on fire."

Doug leaned back in his chair. "He burns the bodies to cover his tracks. And that's worked for him for a very long time. But now we're on to him. And we're going to catch this animal."

Twenty-Four

Sara's Apartment

Adam had been awake most of the night, lying in bed naked with Sara. He admired her body, and listened to her breathing and heartbeat. She was very warm, and actually felt very pleasant. He had now not eaten for a day and a half, and his body temperature was cooling and heart rate was slowing. He would need to eat soon if he was to remain in her company without devouring her. For now, he was under control, and enjoying the new sensations. He ran his hand over her lower back and round buttocks, and she stirred. He smiled as he listened to her waking up. Sleep. Real sleep. He hadn't experienced that since the Battle of Jena, and the concept of day versus night and awake versus sleep was so obscure.

Sara rolled over and faced him, and brushed her thick hair out of her face. She gave him a slow smile and reached out to pull him closer. "*You!*" she exclaimed, "Are amazing. That may have been the single best date of my life.' She paused and pulled back. "I don't mean for that to scare you—you don't have to race out of here or anything. I'm not picking out wedding dresses."

He looked at her, somewhat confused.

"I was kidding, Adam. Relax. But seriously…you are an amazing man. Dinner was perfect, although I think I drank too much, the show was absolutely *spectacular*, and *you*—oh my *God*. I have never come so many times in one night in my life. I think you should have your tongue bronzed."

Adam smiled and thought about that for a moment, then realized she was referring to oral sex. Yes, women did seem to enjoy that. The hardest part was always not ripping through the femoral artery too quickly. The blood was always best when the woman was in a heightened state of arousal, and that technique never failed. Adam rolled her on to her back and slid down her body. She squealed.

"No!" she screamed playfully. "I'm not even awake yet!" He didn't care, he found his ability to control her sexually to be quite enjoyable, and he began to work on her with his tongue again. It wasn't long before she was moaning again, and her blood was pounding in her chest. He could hear the "whoosh" noise of the blood in her femoral arteries, on each side of his ears like headphones, and he fought hard to keep his fangs from extending into the feeding position. Sara came hard, thrashing about the bed as she screamed and threw her legs about. Adam inhaled the chemicals of her body, his mind wandering to thoughts about what she must taste like. It was so *difficult* to keep the animal in. He would need to feed soon. He focused his thoughts on her pleasure, and kept his mind clear of the bloodlust building in his body.

When Sara collapsed back on the bed, completely out of breathe, Adam knew she was done, and he rolled on to his back and thought about how he would broach the subject of having her join him in his current undead condition. Sara had him back in her mouth again, and made him lose his concentration. The girl liked having him inside her, he remembered, and he smiled when she slid up his body and mounted him for a morning session that was every bit as intense as the evening before.

When Sara was completely exhausted, Adam let her fall asleep beside him. Her breathing and heart rate were proof of just how deep a sleep she was enjoying. He watched her for a while, and then decided he should go and take care of his own urges lest he ruin what could be such nice company. He rose quietly, dressed, and slipped out of her apartment. It was Saturday morning, and the street was quiet and bright with sunshine. His skin was beginning to pale, and his eyes were going from deep blue to their silvery color. It was faster than his usual feeding cycle, but perhaps he had used the blood up faster than usual with all of the sexual exertion and stimulation of her company. Adam hustled through the streets, wondering where he could find an easy meal that wouldn't raise suspicion on such a pretty, bright day.

After an hour of walking, lost in thoughts that spanned a century, Adam found himself in a very small park in a quiet residential neighborhood. It was still early for a weekend, and there was almost no activity on the street. Adam stopped and closed his eyes. He smelled the air deeply, listened hard, and cocked his head. He was like a bird listening for worms under the soil. He stood motionless, feeling a heartbeat nearby—it was coming from the park. He walked slowly and quietly until he saw the homeless man sleeping on a park bench. He frowned. The homeless were his least favorite meals. They were dirty and smelled foul. Their blood was full of alcohol and drugs most of the time, and he could practically taste the diseases in them. He recalled spitting a worm out of a mouthful of blood from one of them and made a sour face. Adam glanced around. There was no one else around.

He walked up quickly to the sleeping man, curled up in the fetal position on the green wooden bench and let his talons slide out. His mouth filled up with teeth as they moved into their feeding position. He could feel the lust for blood building up inside, but he didn't like being so out in the open. Adam grabbed the man by the throat, his talons cutting deep into the man's larynx, making him incapable of screaming. With the strength of many men, Adam dragged the man into the cover of some trees and low shrubs and pushed him against the ground, his knee in the man's stomach.

The homeless man, maybe fifty years old but looking much older, was gurgling in shock and horror as he looked up to see what must have been the Grim Reaper himself. Adam leaned in and bit deeply into the man's throat, his hot blood exploding into Adam's mouth. As Adam's eye's rolled back in total bliss, he pictured Sara's naked body, remembered her delicious smells and tastes, and sucked the man dry within a few moments. He finished and looked around him. What to do with the body? He was getting careless. Near the bench there were two small dumpsters, one for recyclables and one for regular trash. He picked up the man, now much lighter, having been drained of his blood and bodily fluids, and rushed to the dumpster. He shoved him deep inside and covered him with trash, closed the top, and rushed out of the quiet park. The taste of the man was warm and nourishing, although not any special delicacy. At least it would keep him under control as he tried to figure out a way to bring Sara into his world.

Twenty-Five

Adam's Lair

Adam wiped off his face and moved quickly back to his own apartment. Once there, he showered, knowing he would stink of the old homeless man, and wanted to see Sara again as soon as possible. As he took off his clothes and walked towards his bathroom, his cell phone rang. There was only one person on Earth who knew his number, and he smiled.

"Well, hello," he said.

"Hey you—where did you go? Am I humped and dumped?" she asked. Adam could hear the smile in her voice.

"Of course not, Sara. You looked so peaceful sleeping. I thought you needed your rest."

"Yeah, well, someone wore me out. My God, Adam. I slept like a rock. You are amazing. Don't get a big head or anything, but I have never had a night like last night. You are *amazing*."

He smiled, genuinely happy to know he had pleased her. It was interesting to him, to feel something human again. It brought emotions that made him sad, but also made him excited and hungry for more of her. "I would say exactly the same thing. In all these years, you alone have made me feel so…" He realized he was thinking out loud. He was about to say "human" when he caught himself. Sara giggled on her end of the phone.

"Yeah, because you are *so* much older than me! *'In all these years*", she said, imitating his voice as best she could. "I make you feel so *what*?"

He smiled. "Hungry." He said quietly.

"Oh my," she said as sexy as she could. "And aren't you the naughtiest man I ever met. And I kind of like it—a lot," she added. "So do I get a second date, or was this a wham-bam-thank you, ma'am?" She hated to sound so hung up on him already, but he really had rocked her world, and she wanted to see him as soon as possible.

"I would love to see you again. Tonight, even."

"*Reeeeeally…*" she said, again trying to sound as alluring as possible.

"Really."

"Well, last night you were obviously trying very hard to impress me, so tonight I will do my best to impress you. How about I make us an intimate little dinner at my place, just the two of us?"

He almost said yes, and then remembered his minor problem with dining. "I'm afraid I can't do dinner. I have some work I need to attend to. I wouldn't be able to see you until almost nine. You go on and eat, and I'll come by after that?"

"You are just trying to use me for sex aren't you?" she asked jokingly. "Well, I can make a late supper."

"No, no food," he said. "The only thing I want to eat is you."

. . .

ADAM SHOWERED AND DRESSED. HE looked in the mirror. He looked
so human. His skin was warm and had human color, and his eyes were
deep blue. He actually wanted to look human…to look *attractive* to a
human. He laughed at himself. Then he felt the cold feeling of sadness
as he remembered the huge separation between them. They could never
truly be together until she knew his secret. Until she knew and wanted
to be just like him. Or until he just went ahead and made her like him
whether she wanted to be or not. And could he even do it?

Adam left his apartment and walked to a pet store. He purchased a
dog that someone had sold back to the store because they were moving
to an apartment that didn't allow dogs. It was an older dog, a female
named Misty that was a mutt, but good natured. When Adam asked
to buy the dog, the pet shop owner saw the way the dog cowered from
the man, but didn't comment. Two hundred bucks was two hundred
bucks, and the dog was "used" and hard to sell. The man gave Adam
the dog on a leash, and Adam pulled the dog out of the store with him.
It had been a "less than emotional" purchase, and the owner hoped
that the man wouldn't hurt the sweet old dog. He watched the dog
walk out, tail between its legs, after the man that pulled it along.

Adam walked back to his apartment and as he got close, realized
that dogs weren't allowed in his building either. He picked the dog
up under his arm, wrapped his coat around it, and walked quickly
inside. He made it to his room unnoticed and closed the door behind
him. He put the pooch down and she immediately moved away from
him, backing into a corner of the room. She was growling—she was

cowering. Adam smiled.

"Come, Misty. I am going to show you how to live forever. That's *seven* forevers in dog years," he joked. He moved quietly across the room, his talons and teeth sliding out as the dog whined in fear, smelling death moving towards it. Adam had eaten a few dogs in his early years. Dogs and many other small animals. But they were no substitute for human blood. Adam sat on the floor and pulled the dog into his lap. He stroked the dogs fur, calming her down until she was panting, her ears still pinned back on her head. Her tail was still between her legs. Adam closed his eyes and thought about the Battle of Jena. He tried to remember the attack of that creature in the forest—the breath in his lungs…the blood in his mouth. He leaned down and pulled the dogs head back, and quickly opened its throat with one of his long claws. The dogs legs started kicking involuntary as it felt itself mortally wounded, and then Adam's mouth was on the dogs open throat. He exhaled slowly into its lungs, and made himself vomit up some of the warm sticky blood that curdled in his stomach.

Disgusting air and blood flooded the dog's senses as it kicked and slowly died. Adam blew into its lungs a few more times, feeling the dogs chest expand like he was blowing up a balloon. He dropped the dog and moved away from it, sitting on the couch as it bled slowly onto his wooden floor. The dog's legs twitched a few times and then went silent. The dog's long tongue slid out of its mouth and the dogs' eyes went dull and lifeless. Adam watched intently, feeling the anger build up inside him. What had he done wrong?

With the dead dog still lying in the middle of his floor, Adam got up and walked to the corner of his room, where he squatted with his back against the corners and his arms wrapped around his shins, his chin on his knees. He closed his eyes and thought back to the woods that day in Jena. What had the creature done differently? Could the curse not be given to a dog? His thoughts wandered through the sea of time, and he was lost.

Hours passed as Adam crouched in the corner bat-like, silently remembering a hundred and fifty years of his experience in the world. The whining of a dog snapped him out of trance.

Misty was awake, but not looking anything like the dog that had been so cute in the pet store. The fuzzy dog with soft brown eyes looked rabid. Its fur was matted and crusty with dried blood. Her ears were still pinned back, but the eyes that had gone dim hours before were now bright—bright red. The animal's teeth seemed to have grown longer, and she was foaming at the mouth, a low growl coming out of her throat. Apparently, the animal didn't like being dead.

Adam smiled broadly. "Welcome to my world," he said quietly to the dog. The dog hunched its shoulder and growled more menacingly. "Shhh," said Adam as he approached the dog, now at full growl. As he got closer, the small dog leapt at him, aiming at his throat. Adam raised his forearm to protect himself, and the dog's long fangs sank into his arm. He screamed in pain, shocked by the strength of the small animal, and the fact that it actually caused him so much agony. He let his own talons slide out and grabbed the dog by the back of its neck. It was wildly clawing and growling at him, as he held it in midair. He looked at the animal's face. "This must be what I look like when I am feeding," he thought to himself. He was so curious about the animal. What would it do if he let it out on the street? He didn't want to kill it. He had created it, like the creature had created him. It struggled and tried to get free of Adam's clawed hand, snapping its teeth at Adam, completely wild. Adam made a sad face. He couldn't let it go. It might bring attention to him, and he couldn't allow that. He grabbed the animal's head with his other clawed hand and pulled as hard as he could, ripping the head off of the undead beast.

The head continued to snap and try and growl, but with no air behind the growl, no sound came out. The legs continued to claw at the air for several minutes, until Adam was tired of his experiment, and he ripped the animal into small pieces until they stopped moving. His arm throbbed. It was bleeding from holes made by the creature's fangs. Surprising.

Adam grabbed a garbage bag and picked up the pieces of dog and threw it in, then tied off the plastic bag. He went to the sink and washed off the blood, then tasted it. It was the blood from the homeless man. It was starting to make more sense. When he was fully fed, and the closest he could be to being "alive", he was most vulnerable. When he was dead, bullets and weapons didn't seem to hurt him. Interesting.

Adam cleaned up and then scoured his apartment. He put all the trash in the bag with the dog pieces, and went to the garbage disposal in the hallway. He dropped the bag down the chute, happy that Monday morning was "furnace day" in the building. When Adam went back inside he realized it was after seven at night. The day had gone by in a blur, and he had a date with Sara again. He smiled, knowing that he had the power to make her like himself. He decided he would feed again before he went to see her. Thoughts of her naked body made his blood lust stronger, and he needed more time with her. He would find food quickly before he went to see her.

Twenty-Six

Is it called a "Man" Hunt?

Sergeant Ruiz, Lt. Joe Alexander, Captain Tim Rosetto and Special Agent Doug Patmore piled into Doug's brown sedan and rode uptown to the 30th precinct where four former gang bangers were now in black plastic bags, lying in refrigerated drawers in the morgue.

"You think we can call it a man hunt?" asked Roy, to no one in particular.

"We can't go public with this, I told you that," said Doug from the driver's seat.

"No, I mean, if we ever *did*. Could we call it a '*man*' hunt. I think it's more like being on safari, trying to kill some wild animal or something. It's more like a '*Thing* Hunt'," replied Roy.

Doug looked at him from his rear view mirror, but didn't say anything.

"He's got a point," said Lt. Alexander from the passenger seat. (They had given Tim the rear seat, since Doug's onboard computer and radio made the front passenger seat a little tight for his huge frame. He was big even for the back seat.) "From what I've seen, I am not sure I'd call this guy a 'man', either. This is some fucked up shit."

They arrived at the 30th precinct and went to the morgue in the basement crime lab. A middle-aged doctor greeted them, exchanging banter with Tim, who was an old acquaintance. The doctor pulled a drawer out from the wall of deceased and unzipped a black bag. What was left of a young Latino male was beyond disgusting. All three cops made a groan and grimaced, Doug never reacted.

"You should have seen him when he came in—before I cleaned him up," said the doc.

"Jesus Christ," said Roy under his breath. "This is *after* you cleaned him up?"

"He is the most intact of the four. You can see them also, if you wish. They've all been burned very badly, but this one had enough flesh to be able to discern some of the wounds. You had alerted us to be on the lookout for animal-looking bite marks. This young man had been attacked and partially eaten before being set on fire."

"I hope he was dead first," said the lieutenant, thinking back to the skulls in the warehouse.

"He most certainly was. He is missing his heart and most of his liver. He was drained of his blood. I mean, completely drained. And then he was tossed into a dumpster with his buddies and burned. There were a few areas of undamaged skin, and these guys had enough gang tattoos on record to help with identification. All four of them were Latin Kings from 146th Street. They all had long rap sheets, and all four had done some time. The city isn't suffering a huge loss by any means, but I am worried about whatever could have done this to four strong men who knew how to fight."

"You and everybody else," said Tim softly.

"There was something interesting I thought you'd want to know about. There was a weapon recovered from the crime scene, assumed to be taken off one of these guys. There was no blood on it, but we did recover some old tissue off the blade and in the handle. We ran DNA tests to see if it matched any unsolved cases, and sure enough, it did. But this must have been his grandfather's knife or something that was kept in a safe place for a few decades. The DNA matches to an unknown suspect in another unsolved case."

"Yeah?" asked Joe softly.

"From 1966," said the doc with a puzzled look on his face.

"We're getting closer," said Doug. "So help me God, I am going to catch this animal."

Twenty-Seven

Sara

Adam got to Sara's brownstone a little after nine. He had taken the subway downtown to the Seaport and meandered around until he found a vagrant in the park, separated from the others. He fed quickly and quietly, and dumped the body into the water with a large stone tied to the body as he had done many times in the past. He then returned home, cleaned up and changed, and went back across town to her brownstone.

Sara answered the door with a glass of wine in her hand, and smiled. She invited him in, handed him the glass of wine, and kissed him on the mouth. "I was afraid you weren't going to show up," she said as she took his coat.

"I'm not *that* late!" he replied with his most charming voice.

"I guess I'm over anxious. I should learn to play hard to get," she said. She had flirting eyes that twinkled in the dim light of her foyer. "Come on in."

He followed her in, and panicked when he saw a large tray of very fancy appetizers laid out for him with a glass of wine. He could feel himself getting angry. It wasn't her fault—she was trying so hard to please him, but this was very difficult. He was angry at not being able to eat regular food and appreciate her work on his behalf. He was angry at not being able to drink wine and feel any warmth or pleasure from it. He looked at her and heard her heart pounding. At least he was able to enjoy her.

"I made us a little snack," she said, walking towards her beautiful assortment of food. "I even made you some fresh sushi, although I know it won't be as good as Kazu's." She walked over and grabbed a piece and tried to pop it into his mouth. He grabbed her hand and leaned in and licked the tuna, pulling off a small piece with his teeth. He could get *that* down…but not the rice. "I told you," he said leaning closer to her, "there is only one thing I want to eat here."

He kissed her deeply and she wrapped her arms around him, melting against his strong frame. "Adam!" she gasped when they broke their kiss. "Come on—sit and have something to eat first. I don't want to just be your fuck buddy…I want to get to know you…"

He picked her off her feet like she was weightless and carried her back to her bedroom. "You'll get to know me. But first, I want to know you…every inch." He kissed her as he carried her, and she didn't resist.

After they had made love for over an hour, Sara was soaked in sweat and completely spent. She looked at Adam and shook her head. "I don't know if it's just because the sex is *so* fucking good or not, but God, Adam, you *really* get to me."

"So maybe I get a third date?" he asked. Unlike Sara, he was not out of breath or sweaty at all. He felt the rush of power from his overfeeding the last few days, and was enjoying the warmth of Sara's body and the pounding of her pulse.

She pulled herself closer to him and whispered, "You get as many dates as you want…"

Twenty-Eight

Sgt. Roy Ruiz had left the precinct for the night, showering and changing at the station and stopping for a beer and quick bite at the local cop bar. He lived near the precinct and walked almost every day. By the time he had eaten and walked home, it was almost midnight. He was almost at his apartment when his cell phone rang showing Tim's number.

"Don't tell me you're still up working?" he said with a laugh.

"Is this Roy Ruiz?" asked an unfamiliar female voice.

"Yeah, who is this?"

"This is Rachael Clark, over at Mount Sinai. I believe you are friends with Tim Rosetto?"

"Yeah, is he okay?" asked Roy, now stopped in his tracks.

"Well, he's had a heart attack. He's in ICU getting ready for surgery and he asked that I call you."

Roy was now running as he was talking, looking frantically for a taxi. "He gonna' make it?" he asked as he ran down the street.

"The doctors are with him now running tests. He is stable, and I am sure he will be fine. He just wanted us to contact you, said you'd be worried if you didn't hear from him tomorrow."

Roy thanked her, hailed a cab, and ordered the cabby to fly across town.

They arrived at the hospital twenty minutes later, and Roy paid the driver and sprinted upstairs. He used his shield to get upstairs to ICU and found Tim in his room surrounded by staff and a cop from the Sixth. Tim was groggy, but lifted a hand slightly when he saw Roy.

"Be quick," said a nurse with a hard look at him. "We need to take him over to surgery. You have two minutes."

"Hey Pisano," said Tim in a faint voice. "Fucking donuts attacked me." He smiled slightly. "I'm sorry to leave you to do all my work, but it looks like I'm gonna' be out for a while. You need to catch this fucking ghoul while I get sponge baths from cute nurses," he said as he smiled at a young nurse nearby.

"What happened?" asked Roy, scared by the number of tubes and machines attached to his friend.

"Usual symptoms, you know—I passed out and grabbed my left arm on the way down screaming. One of my guys at the Sixth was with me, and saved my fat ass. Guess I have a diet in my future."

"Jesus, Tim. Listen, you need anything, you let me know, okay?" he asked, as the nurse came back pointing to her watch.

"Your friend has a date with a surgeon right now. You can speak with him later in the afternoon tomorrow."

Roy gave Tim's arm a squeeze and told him to hang tough, then left as they rushed Tim down a hall to surgery. He grabbed another nurse and tried to get more specific information from her, but she wasn't much help. He left her his cell number and asked her to call him after the surgery. He walked downstairs and hailed another cab, almost falling asleep in the back seat as he thought about his new friend laying on the gurney.

"I'll catch him, Tim" he said to himself as his head rocked around in the bumpy cab.

Twenty-Nine

Sunday Morning

When Sara woke up, Adam wasn't in bed, and she thought he had left again. She moaned as she stretched, a long, very happy stretch after a very deep sleep. She had enjoyed the best sex of her life for two nights in a row, and had found the most interesting man she had ever met. She rolled on her side and curled up, feeling warm under her covers.

"Adam?" she asked with a start. She sat up in her bed, alarmed, as she spotted Adam squatting in the corner of her room, his arms wrapped around his legs and his chin resting on his chest. For a moment, she thought he was asleep, but his eyes were open. "Adam? Are you okay?"

His face changed, from a blank stare back to his charming smile. He quickly thought of an answer for her, speaking from his strange position in the corner. "I'm sorry, Sara," he said quietly as he stood up.

"I didn't mean to startle you. I was watching you sleep. You looked so, I don't know, beautiful and content. I guess I nodded off."

Sara threw her covers open, showing him her naked body. "Well, come over here and you can see better." She was smiling at him. He had been watching her for a long time? Maybe he was as smitten as she was, she thought to herself. Adam crossed the small room and slid into her warm bed, feeling her body heat and smelling her skin. He got on top of her and kissed her.

"I didn't brush my teeth!" she said with a laugh. He ignored her and kissed her, tasting her breath but not finding it unpleasant. (This coming from a creature whose own breath smelled like death when he was hungry.) He continued to kiss her, and she wrapped her legs around him, feeling his strong body with her soft hands. She reached down and repositioned him so he could enter her, and the two of them made love slowly and passionately. Adam was surprised by how much he enjoyed the act of sex with this human. Since his few days with Renee, his only real pleasure had been during feeding. And although he had sexually abused some of his victims, it was done more to increase their fear or pain, or an attempt to feel more human. This Sara woman was different. She made him feel an emotion he might even consider to be like "love", whatever *that* was. He knew she made him feel more human than he had since Renee, or perhaps even back to Jena, when he *was* human.

He was lost in this stream of consciousness when his partner's orgasms began and brought him back to the present. He looked down at her, her eyes closed, lost in pleasure, and he watched her carotid artery moving with each heartbeat. He felt his mouth filling with teeth and began thrusting against her as hard as he could to shake off the need to rip her throat open. His hard thrusts made Sara scream out, bringing her another wave of pleasure. She had no way to know he was only trying to keep himself from ripping her to pieces and eating her organs as he sucked her blood. He roared once, accidently, as he fought off the urge, and she smiled and screamed with him, a long "Yes! Come inside me!" He relaxed and lay on her, and she wrapped her arms around him.

"God, Adam," she managed to say between breaths.

Adam wondered where God was. And why he had cursed him to be alone in the world while someone he wanted to be with was lying beneath him. He rolled off of her and let her wrap herself around him while she recovered.

"I'll make you breakfast in bed," she whispered. "Anything you want…"

Adam sighed. It must be so nice for humans to eat together. Share a coffee. Sit and share each other's company. Not the great pleasure of feeding the way he did, which was so much more than simply "eating", but still, the companionship of it all. It made him feel so horribly lonely. This time, maybe for the first time ever, it didn't lead to anger—only sorrow.

"What's the matter, Adam? You looked so sad just then. Is everything okay?"

He turned his face at her, his dark blue eyes shining at her. "I feel quite differently around you," he said, not sure how he would explain anything to her.

She rubbed his chest. "I know what you mean, I think. I mean, I hope. We hardly know each other, and we're already sleeping together. And, oh my God, it's been unbelievable—and even though I hardly know you, I just, I don't know, I can't stop thinking about you."

He looked at her sadly again.

"I'm sorry—I don't mean to sound so serious. I mean, we hardly know each other, right?" She felt vulnerable and tried to put up some type of wall quickly.

He reached over and pulled her close, and she hugged him. "It has been very interesting," he said, matter of factly. "There is so much to tell you about, but where to begin?" He was talking to himself as much as he was speaking to her.

"Well, that will be half the fun, right? Getting to know each other. We'll have to spend more time together." Then she made a pouty face. "But then work starts again tomorrow, and the party is over."

"What do you do?" he asked, curious to know more about the woman that was changing the way he felt about his lot in life—or afterlife.

She laughed. "This is so bizarre. I know you won't believe me, but I don't just hop into bed with strange men. I have been out with guys three or four times and barely kissed them. We're having sex like porn stars and you don't even know what I do. I don't know what *you* do either, come to think of it."

"You first."

"Well, I am a financial analyst for a multinational investment bank here in New York. Been with the same company since I graduated college. I went to Rutgers. And you?"

Adam thought for a moment. "I was in the army for a long time," he began.

She put her finger on the scar on his chest, made during the American Civil War over a hundred years earlier. "Is that how you got *this*?" she asked.

"Yes."

I saw a scar on your back, too. Did it go right through?"

"Yes, it did."

"God, that must have hurt," she said, caressing his very old scar.

"I hardly remember," he said.

"You traveled a lot in the army? Is that where you learned to speak so many languages?" she asked, leaning over to kiss his scar.

"Yes. I traveled quite a bit while in uniform." He wasn't lying; he just hadn't mentioned it had begun in the early 19th century.

"And what do you do now?" she asked, lightly kissing his chest between questions.

Adam had pondered this discussion while crouching in her corner over the course of the night while she slept. "I do some work for the government, Department of Defense. I'm afraid I can't really talk about it too much. Sorry."

"Hmm…a mystery man. A secret agent, maybe? I knew you were fascinating. Maybe I can torture you and get it out of you…" she said with her version of an "evil smile".

"I would only give you name, rank and serial number," he joked, his mind racing with thoughts of torture that he had seen, and participated in.

"How about I make you some coffee? Then you can spill your guts."

He thought about her choice of words. "Spill your guts". He had spilled many over the years. There was no remorse about it, he needed to eat. To survive. And it was who and what he was. And in those moments when he fed, he didn't curse his condition—he reveled in it. There was simply no greater pleasure than sucking the living blood out of a human. The life energy that sprayed into his mouth was beyond any human pleasure, even those he gave Sara in her bed. He could never really explain just how intense and thrilling it was to feel his body fill up with life and hot nourishment as he shredded his pray. He wanted Sara to feel it with him. To join him in his 'undeath'. To be his partner and see the world. He could teach her so much. He could be her mentor and…he laughed and wondered if he still had a soul? He would have called her his soul mate…but alas, he feared his soul was long gone, left in the woods of Jena.

"*Hello?*" she said playfully, knocking on his chest. "Is anyone home?"

"Sorry", he said. "I can't stay. Coffee in bed would be wonderful, I'm sure. But I really need to get home."

"Oh," she said quietly. He could feel her disappointment. It made him angry again. How could it ever work with her until she was undead with him? His rage built quietly inside his chest. "It's okay. Maybe we can get together during the week?" she asked quietly, feeling desperate in a way—that maybe he would blow her off and she would feel like an idiot for sharing her bed with a stranger.

"That would be very nice," he said, and kissed the top of her head.

She reached down and started caressing him. "How soon did you have to leave?" she asked.

"I have a few minutes," he said and inhaled her pheromones. The girl did seem to enjoy sex, he thought to himself. And it *was* very human and pleasant.

Thirty

Roy woke up after nine, very late for him. He was usually up at seven or so, did his thing for a few hours during the day, and was at work by one-thirty to work out and shower and change into his uniform for roll call at three. He had been up late the night before, having run to the hospital, and then having a crappy night's sleep when he got home. He sat up and checked his cell phone. He had a voice mail. Damn. He must have slept through the ring after all. He called his voicemail and a nurse from the hospital left a message saying that Tim was out of surgery and would be recuperating from a triple bypass for a couple of days in ICU.

He was relieved. At least his corpulent friend had survived the heart attack. He called Captain Ammiano and got his voicemail, so he left a message about Tim. He would now have to do more of the legwork. Not that the LT or captain weren't helping, but they had a bunch of other stuff to do as well, and other than FBI Agent Patmore, Roy would have to pick up Tim's slack. He wondered if Tim would ever return to work. He called a florist and sent flowers to Tim's room, along with a box of doughnuts he knew Tim wouldn't be allowed to eat, but would at least give him a chuckle.

Roy called Patmore's number that he had stored in his cell phone. Doug saw Roy's name pop up and answered with a "Good morning, Roy."

"Hey, Doug. Just thought I'd give you some bad news. Tim…"

"Yeah, I heard. He's going to be fine. Triple bypass went well. He's in a great hospital. Although I think his days as a cop are over."

"How did you find out so fast?"

"Um, *hello*? We're the FBI, Roy…I'm kidding. One of the guys in his precinct called me this morning right before you did."

"Anything new?"

"There's always something new. What time are you going in? I thought you worked three to eleven?"

"Yeah, well, I used to. With Tim out of commission and something eating people in Midtown, I thought I might go in early."

"Get dressed and I'll pick you up in thirty minutes downstairs."

"You know where I live?"

"Roy…"

"Yeah, yeah, I forgot,,, you're the FBI." He hung up and hit the shower. He dressed in plainclothes and eyed his spare bulletproof vest. He wore it on those rare occasions when working plainclothes, but didn't think it would help against a man-eating monster and didn't bother. By the time he got downstairs, Doug was parked by the fire hydrant. Roy hopped in and they sped off, heading uptown.

"We're we going?" asked Roy.

"I'm taking you to *my* office. I have almost two years worth of files on this thing. I can't really bring the whole taskforce into my office, but I'll see if I can catch you up a little better."

They drove to an underground garage and parked, then took an elevator up to the tenth floor of the building. They entered a sealed corridor, and Doug used a swipe card to unlock a series of doors.

Roy was somewhat shocked. "This whole floor is FBI?" he asked.

"Yeah, and keep that to yourself," Doug said. "This is a New York special services sub-station. We don't advertise this location, and we don't take anyone from the public in here. We still have a *couple* of secrets, I guess."

Doug said a few hellos as they passed folks in the hallways, and then entered his office. It was tiny. His desk and computers looked brand new, and file cabinets, some with combination locks like vaults filled the walls. Other than the desk chair and two small chairs on the other side of the desk, no one else was fitting in the office.

"You see why I can't have the whole taskforce up here now?" asked Doug.

"Or Tim," said Roy, wondering how his buddy was feeling.

Doug sat and dialed into his computer after inviting Roy to sit. "You'll want to see this. I had the docs down at the lab work some of the bite wounds and teeth models. We have 3-D models of some of the wounds, even from old cases. I know your police crime lab has a bite model, and it's pretty good, but our guys pulled some old files and built some models of the attack victims based on photos and measurements in the coroners' reports. I'll go steal us some bad coffee. Sit here and use the mouse the scroll around the models…these commands here will move it in 3D for you." Doug left and Roy sat down and moved the model of some prehistoric jaws armed with horrific teeth. He was still lost in thought when Doug returned with two coffees and some sugar and creamer packs, which he put on his desk.

"Nasty stuff, huh?" he asked Roy. Roy was still turned the pictures around in different views.

"Unfuckingbelievable, man. How many DBs did you go through?" he asked.

"Those models represent almost a hundred victims. The oldest dates back to the sixties. I have DNA matches to almost a dozen crime scenes, including the most recent one we're working together. I also have fingerprints that go back to the forties. This thing, and I do say "thing", not person in this little room of mine only, has been around for a long time, Roy. I can't speak to a whole group the way I can talk to you about this, because everyone will think I'm nuts, but you and I are going to catch this fucking monster."

Roy grunted. He noticed that Doug, unlike his cop buddies, rarely cursed. This thing really pissed him off.

"So you *must* have some theories. I mean, you've been doing this case fulltime for almost two years. You must have something you aren't talking about. How does a guy do what this guy does and not get caught?"

"That's just it. For years, this guy left almost no trace. But I think he's getting sloppy. I mean, sure, our techniques are a heck of a lot better now than they were a decade ago, but he's also leaving a lot more evidence. I went through files some months back regarding bodies recovered from the water around the city. Lots of references to "damage from sea life"—like sharks had been eating the victims. You see any sharks in the Hudson River? I think this guy was eating his victims and dropping them into the water for years."

"Hard to tell on floaters…" said Roy, looking at a series of grisly pictures on Doug's computer.

"To a degree, yes. But there were teeth marks on some of the bones that I showed to an oceanographer. He said they weren't from any fish. Same canine incisors and tooth structure as the others. He said they were mammal, most likely primate, feline or canine. In other words, he had no idea, but knew enough to say it wasn't a fish. Fish have hundreds of teeth, and they don't have fangs. And there's more."

Doug closed and locked his door and sat in the guest chair with Roy still seated at his desk. "Listen Roy, I need someone to work with on this case that I can trust. And I don't mean 'trust' like not talk about details to reporters; I mean trust, like, that you understand I am not insane. When we spoke about keeping an open mind at that first briefing—I really meant it. I am pretty sure your Heather Connell 'gets it', too. But *you* need to get it, Roy. I'm going to share some things with you that need to stay here for a while. A group of two can handle this info. A room full of cops? No way. They'll get drunk and talk shit in public, and the public's reaction will range from outrage at the waste of taxpayer money, to total panic, to long lines of whackos screaming 'I told you so'…"

Roy leaned back in Doug's chair and folded his arms. "Okay, Agent Patmore. You have my undivided attention. Out with it."

Doug looked at him and rubbed his face, tried to pick a place to begin, and then said, "Here goes. The case you call Goth Girl. She had skin tissue under her fingernails. Your crime lab said it wasn't viable tissue. I took it to my guy. I told him what he was looking for, sort of. Make a very long complicated story short—this tissue was from a corpse. Meaning, the tissue was dead when she got it under her fingernails."

"She was into some weird Goth shit. Was she having sex with corpses or something? Like necrophilia?" Roy's face was contorted in disgust.

"Let me finish. I had the DNA run through a few high-end computers we have. Top of the line systems we have used for everything from identifying United States servicemen recovered in Vietnam sixty years after they were killed, to helping with 9-11 trace evidence. You follow me?"

"Yeah. If there's a trace of DNA, you'll find it."

"Not just *find* it—*positively identify* it against a huge database of DNA samples that includes *millions* of people. It's one thing to say, yes, it was human dead tissue. It's another thing to say it was the dead tissue from dozens of people."

"I'm not sure I follow you?" asked Roy.

"That's okay, just listen. Yesterday, a sanitation worker found a DB in a dumpster uptown. Nice little residential park. The guy was a homeless man, and was somewhat known in the area. He'd been chased out plenty of times, but he liked the neighborhood. Not many gangbangers to kick his ass or rob him. Anyway, I saw the coroner's report, and I am 100% sure he was eaten by our creature. Now pay attention. At the bite marks, there was some foreign tissue, as well as foreign tissue in the claw marks. Like…" Doug closed his eyes. "Let's just say maybe the thing that was feeding on him hadn't brushed his teeth or filed his nails or something from the *last* feeding…you with me?"

Roy shook his head yes, a look of disgust still on his face.

Doug continued. "So I had our best guys running DNA trace on the bits and pieces. Roy—this is so fucked up. I got hits on those four dead gang bangers uptown that were slashed and burned. Are you following me?"

Roy sat back and connected the dots, and the logic was almost too disgusting to repeat aloud. He spoke slowly, choosing each word painfully. "So…you are saying, the lab results conclude that the victim of another one of these attacks was *not* attacked by the four gangbangers, but that whatever killed *them, also* killed this homeless man? This 'thing' had killed the four gangbangers, and had some leftover shit in his teeth or nails that he left in the recovered body you just found. "

"In a nutshell."

"That's some fucked up shit, Doug."

"Yeah. Now, let's go back to Goth Girl. The DNA under her fingernails was from several dead males. And unless she was in fact having sex with corpses, it becomes very difficult to explain. Especially when one of the corpses would have been dead twenty years and beyond having skin on it. Unless she kept it in a deep freeze somewhere, and we don't have any evidence to suggest that."

They sat blankly staring at each other.

"Do you want to try and explain what the fuck you just said to me?" asked Roy.

"Nope. Because I might doubt my sanity. I would much rather have you explain it back to me based solely on the facts that I have presented to you."

Roy sat back in the chair and looked out the window overlooking the city. Somewhere out there, there was something beyond explanation that was feeding on human beings. Roy took a deep breath. "Okay," he said very quietly. "Let's forget what we think we know about human beings for a second and just go strictly by the evidence. I'm not even going to look at you when I am talking because this is completely absurd."

"Welcome to my world," said Doug quietly as he picked up a black coffee.

"We have a young woman, sexually assaulted and viciously murdered in her apartment. She has been bitten and drained of most of her blood. She apparently scratched her attacker. The skin under her nails turns out to be from several dead bodies. Am I following along so far?"

"You must be doing great—it sounds insane."

"Okay, so more than one guy is under her nails, and you say one of the guys was dead twenty years ago. How do you know *that*?"

"Because we have a match to a 1991 unsolved murder case. It wasn't here in the city. The FBI had a file open because the missing person was a woman who was living in Pennsylvania and the body was over the state line in upstate New York. Young woman named Darci West. She was a dancer at some hole in the wall bar in Philly and went missing. She had a couple of priors for solicitation, dope, and shoplifting. Nothing big. Anyway, she turns up at a cabin in upstate New York along with two other women's bodies. The hunter that found them was a big strong guy, you know, an outdoorsman. He was practically out of his mind when he drove back down the mountain and called police. He ended up shooting himself in 1993. Most of his friends said he never got over what he saw. I saw the crime scene photos and I understand how he could snap after that."

"Our killer ate them, I presume?" asked Roy, feeling queasy.

"Yes, partially. But he apparently tortured them first. It was a huge case at the time. We spent huge amounts of money and came up with nothing. State Police, FBI, local cops—no one could catch a break. Whoever did it, just disappeared. But evidence at the scene was processed and kept in the FBI central system. The victims had tissue under their nails, which didn't make any sense at the time, but looking back now, I think I understand some of it."

"Such as?" asked Roy.

One of the victims had tissue from the other two under her nails. It was assumed they had fought each other, or been made to fight each other, or tie each other up or something like that. Knowing what I know now…" he hesitated. "I think the killer ate the first two, ingested their DNA, and then ate the third woman later. She fought back as best she could and scratched him. She got skin under her nails from him, which now contained DNA from the two women he had consumed." Doug sat back and folded his arms.

Roy spoke quietly. "You see how I am staring out the window and not looking at you?"

"Yup."

"I'm just gonna' stare at your window for a little while."

"Yup." Doug sipped his coffee.

Thirty-One

Adam's Lair

dam had returned home Sunday morning after enjoying "sins of the flesh" with Sara. "Sins of the flesh" she had called it, jokingly. He wondered about *his* sins with flesh. Sins? No, just food. If God had thought it was a sin, He would have protected Olmer that night in the woods. Adam was sulking a bit. He stripped and squatted in the corner, his arms wrapped around his legs with his chin on his knees. He could still smell Sara all over him, and it made him happy and angry at the same time. He remembered enough about being human to know that there was a connection between Sara and him. Something emotional, physical, *human*. His feelings were changing—becoming painful. He could feel anger creeping into his body again, his mouth filling with teeth. His face tightened as his fangs started to slide into the position that meant horrific death to all that saw them.

Adam forced the anger away, clenching and unclenching his hands, compelling himself to relax. He refocused on the dog he had killed, reanimated, and killed again. He had the power to kill, but he also had the power to create more beings like himself. It had never occurred to him prior to meeting Sara that he could make others into whatever *he* was, and he never really knew the answer to that question. *What* was he? In one hundred and fifty years of reading and watching bad Hollywood movies to try and better understand himself, he was no closer today than he was a hundred years ago. Certainly, he was no Hollywood vampire. He walked in the day without fear of sunlight, and churches did him no harm. He didn't fear a cross, although it did anger him when he thought about how God had abandoned him. He had once thought about massacring a church full of priests to send a message to God, but was afraid of the publicity it might cause.

Adam inhaled deeply. His body reeked of sex. Sara was such a pleasure as a physical companion. While she couldn't compete with the feeling of feeding, her warm smile and laughter was so human and satisfying in its own way. He thought about the day when he saw her for the first time. He had only wanted the coat. He remembered the other girl and her cheap coat, and stood up. He walked to his closet and pulled it from a hanger. It still stunk of cigarettes and cheap perfume. He recalled the girl's white skin and stunned face as she laid spread out on her bed. He wished Sara could have seen that picture. She would have wanted to photograph it. Or would she? Perhaps she would be horrified? She was human. Kind. Loving. She could never understand his need to feed on humans. She would loath him and fear him and scream in terror the way they all did. Her body would make adrenaline and push extra oxygen into her bloodstream, and she would taste so alive. Her blood would be crisp and hot and full of life. Adam realized he was standing naked, rubbing the coat against his privates. He smiled at himself. Sara really was waking up another lust in him that had been quite dead since Renee.

Adam threw the coat into the closet and showered off Sara's scent. It would be too much for him all day. He couldn't stand to smell her and begin to want her all day long. If *that* happened, he would call her and she would invite him over, and he would suck every delicious drop of blood out of her until she was dead. No. He needed to control himself. Maybe an extra large meal would calm him down.

Adam stepped into the shower and let the warm water run over him. He used lots of soap that reminded him of the woods near Jena. The same Sandalwood smell as the Japanese restaurant where he had dined with Sara. It reminded him of happy days when he was alive. It reminded him of Sara. He inhaled deeply and closed his eyes under the water. Adam washed with soap thoroughly, thinking about his eating habits of late. He had been eating large meals more frequently. He needed to be more careful. Perhaps it was time for a trip. He had, during his "afterlife", traveled all over the country. He had seen (and eaten) in most of the United States and Canada. The subtle differences in diet had made humans taste differently by region. It lent a whole new meaning to "going out for Chinese or Mexican". Maybe it was time to get out of the city for a few days. But what about Sara?

Adam turned off the water and stepped out, dripping wet. He looked in the mirror at his own naked image. He looked almost exactly as he did that day he died in Jena. He was strong, and as good looking as any other human he had seen. As long as he was well fed. After four or five days, he looked quite dead. His white skin began to look putrefied; his eyes shimmered silvery and devoid of life. His hair would get mangy and matted. And he would no longer be able to keep his teeth and fangs in place. When it was time to feed, to *really* feed out of total *necessity,* there was no keeping the animal under control. At those times, he would never be able to see himself in a mirror. It was too sad to see what he had become. Sara couldn't ever see that. If she did, it would be the last thing she ever saw as a living human.

Adam walked back into his bedroom and squatted back in his corner. He didn't really need to eat yet. He had been gorging himself. But he also didn't want to risk losing control around Sara. He thought about how many victims he had eaten recently in the city. He continued to squat in his corner, and allowed time to pass. He played a frequent mind game, and began counting backwards from his most recent meal. He rarely got beyond a few months. And then, of course, there were those special ones—the ones that would stand out forever. The killing fields of Fredericksburg and Gettysburg. His days during the Great Wars—both of them. There had been so many bodies. So much blood. Everyone was living in the same un-dead world *with* him for *those* years, with dead bodies too numerous to count. He could gorge himself for months and no one would even notice. The bloodlust of *those* days were almost like the sexual promiscuity of young people in their college days, where "anything goes".

Adam smiled in his trancelike state. Beyond his glazed eyes, he could see battlefields with corpses as far as the horizon. He could smell the burnt flesh, the bubbling blood. He remembered putting on the arm band of a Medic once, and feasting on the wounded for weeks during one of his lazier periods. He was eventually discovered eating a wounded soldier, and had to kill several soldiers and all of the wounded within earshot to prevent being caught. He had covered those tracks with a few grenades which were blamed on the enemy. How many years had he lived on the fringe of the battlefield? Dozens? Hundreds? They were too many to count. And it was always the same, anyway. The uniforms and weapons changed, but the misery was constant. Humans loved to kill each other, and those that were only wounded were such easy meals—and *so* plentiful. The bloodlust from the battlefield was intense because of its quantity, but it was the *quality* of the bloodlust that changed when he tired of the noise of battle and switched to the blood of females.

From his beginning days in Jena, Adam had survived by staying near the battlefields and finding those easy meals "on the fringe". Because of the huge quantities to be had there, he fed primarily on soldiers for years. It wasn't for almost ten years that he drained a *woman* of her blood, and he was amazed by the difference.

When feasting on soldiers, he could taste their fear, their intensity and adrenaline from battle. The endorphins from their terrible wounds, and the over oxygenation of their blood as their lungs worked overtime in their panicked state. The strong soldiers had made him stronger, and kept him full of fearless, animal-like energy. When he fed on his first female, it was at a house he had found shelter in shortly after the wars had ended. A family of farmers had allowed him to stay at their barn for a night, taking pity on his bloody uniform. That night, when the father came out to bring him some water and leftover food, Olmer ate him without a moment's hesitation. It had been almost four days, and he was beyond control. Once the animal was out, Olmer moved quickly to the house and ate the farmer's son who was fast asleep. He then moved to the daughter's room. She was asleep as well, and Olmer entered her room to find the pretty teenager under a large comforter. Olmer crept close and smelled the girl. It was so different from all the men he had eaten. Soldiers were a stinky lot—sweat, fear, weapon grease, weeks of grime and bad food, dysentery—he had never known any differently. But this girl, she smelled like flowers and hay.

Olmer had lifted her heavy quilt and slid in bed next to her, then smelled her hair. He moved closer behind her and ran his hands over her body, and that was when she woke up. It was dark in the room. While Olmer could see quite well in the dark, the young girl could not.

"Papa?" she exclaimed. She couldn't imagine who could have slid into her bed. She called her brother's name. Olmer watched her face in the dark. She looked so afraid. He could smell it in her. Fear. It made him need to taste it. When he buried his fangs into her throat, she exploded into his mouth and he made gurgling noises as he slurped and ate her flesh. She tasted wonderfully feminine, and Olmer was delighted with this new sensation. It was that evening when he got rid of the Prussian army uniform, and took the father's clothes. He piled up the family, took whatever was useful or worth money, and burned down their house with them in it. For the next two hundred years, not much changed in his "M.O.".

Adam came back to 2011 with the ringing of his disposable cell phone. Sara. He felt uneasy, but picked up the phone and said hello.

"Hey, you! I thought you were going to call me. Whatcha' doing ?" Sara asked, sounding chipper as usual.

Adam watched the farmhouse in his mind collapse under sparks as flames shot towards the heavens. That young girl had been so delicious. What would Sara taste like…?

"Adam? You there?"

Adam snapped out of his visions. "Sorry, bad connection. Are you working all week?" he asked.

"Of course, unless you are taking me to St. Lucia for the week."

Adam thought about that. Traveling with Sara.

"Adam! I was *kidding*. Hello?"

Adam came back to the present. "It would be nice to travel with you," he said, almost to himself.

She giggled. "Yeah, the beach sounds nice, huh? I'd even wear my teeny weenie bikini for you."

Adam had seen people lying on the beach for hours, burning their skin. While he understood the desire to feel that warmth, there were better ways to get it than burning your skin. "What time do you get off work?" he asked.

"Five-thirty," she said. "I'm supposed to meet my friend Sharon for snacks and a drink after work. I told her all about you. Want to meet us? We're going to Brodsky's right by my office?"

He agreed to meet her, and she gave him instructions on where to meet them. Adam was in a deep quandary. He would enjoy traveling with Sara. He found travel interesting, and had seen so much of the world. He had been content to live in New York, and the food had been plentiful and the lifestyle an easy one. It was easy to simply disappear into the sea of humanity, even if he wasn't human. Sara would be such a good companion. They could live together and he could show her the world that he lived in. If he had a heart that beat with his own blood, it might have ached.

Thirty-Two

Doug's Office

Roy and Doug had spent hours in Doug's tiny office. Roy had called in to the Midtown North Precinct and told him he was working with Doug out of the precinct, and the LT had excused him from roll call. They had been weaving together evidence from decades of unsolved cases that all had DNA, fingerprints, or other evidence that one way or the other overlapped other "mysterious" cases. When Roy and Doug agreed not to accuse each other of being crazy, and to open their minds to strictly the facts of the evidence as it occurred, they could more easily follow exactly what was actually occurring. It was like a "handoff" of DNA from one crime scene to the next.

After almost four hours without a break, the two of them had constructed a timeline that went case to case in a most bizarre fashion.

Normally, DNA from an original case would appear at a second or third case and the investigator would link the cases together based on one original suspect. In this strange set of circumstances they were assembling, DNA from multiple, seemingly unrelated cases, linked dozens of cases together, even though there should not have been any direct links between those cases or victims.

In the process of their investigation, they apparently solved an age-old, unsolved gang rape and brutal murder. In a terrible crime that occurred in 1995 in New York City, a young woman had been gang raped, sexually assaulted and then brutally dismembered. Based on the crime scene evidence at the time, in particular the DNA evidence recovered from a rape kit and from under the victim's fingernails, it was assumed that four men had raped and then viciously murdered the woman. A week later, when the bodies of two male gang members were recovered at another crime scene, their DNA matched the deceased. It was assumed that these two men had been part of the gang that raped and killed the victim, before being violently murdered themselves. Because the other two contributors of DNA had yet to be found, the case remained "open and unsolved", even though police thought they had found two of the four assailants.

Roy read the same report three times. Finally, he built up the nerve to say what he was thinking to Doug. "Okay, man. Just me and you in this room, right? I want to say what I'm thinking, and not have you give me any shit, all right?"

"Roy, I told you, I have been questioning my sanity for almost two years with this case."

"All right. Let's just pretend for a second, okay? Just humor me. Let's say that this man isn't really a man like you and me. Let's pretend he is some fucking vampire monster. I don't care *what* you call him, but let's just say for the sake of argument that he's a vampire."

"Okay. He's a vampire," said Doug with a calm voice.

"Okay. So he eats and drinks human blood and shit because he needs to, to stay alive for food. So—he consumes the blood, and along with it, the DNA of that human. Then, at the next crime scene, we find *that* DNA. It's *our* vampire-*same guy*—but with the DNA from someone else. He's just passing it on. Don't look at me like I'm crazy," said Roy, almost exasperated.

"I reached this conclusion almost nine months ago, so no, I don't think you're crazy. And I am so happy to hear another human say that out loud I could cry. It's the only thing that makes sense, and trust me, Roy, I have spent a thousand hours on this. The only thing I have a harder time with is the rape kit. The DNA wasn't just in the blood, it was in the semen, too."

"So? Maybe vampires need to get laid, too. And if they do, and they have bodily fluids shooting out of them, it makes sense that it is the same DNA as the stuff in their blood."

"I'm not sure I would use the phrase, 'making sense' anywhere near this investigation," said Doug. "But yeah, I see your point. If we are going to accept that this creature ingests DNA into his body, why not also in his blood and semen. You realize this means we need to pull every unsolved rape case in the city that had a rape kit collected and check it against the data base of every one of these cases."

Roy rubbed his face. "Yeah. Maybe after lunch. My eyes are going to fall out of my head." He looked at his watch. "Shit, man. It's after one. Want to grab some chow?"

"Yeah," said Doug. "But I am thinking of turning vegetarian."

. . .

ROY AND DOUG WALKED DOWN the block and sat down in a small pizza joint that had a counter by the window overlooking the street. Roy spoke between bites of pizza. (Neither of them could even think about a bloody hamburger after all the pictures they had seen that morning.) "You think we'd notice him if he walked by?"

Doug shrugged as he burned the roof of his mouth on his first bite. He wiped his face and drank coke to put the fire out. "I wonder about that. Whether or not he looks like everyone else out there." They spoke in very quiet voices in the loud lunch crowd.

"It would be so much easier if a bat flew by and turned into a guy in a black cape that sounded like Bela Legosi," said Roy. "And I prefer to picture *him*, because that fucker from Bram Stoker's Dracula would have me shitting my pants if I ran into him."

"Yeah. Think this will be like Abbott and Costello meet Dracula?" asked Doug.

"As long as *you* are Costello," said Roy. "Seriously, man. Let's say we get lucky and catch up to this thing. How the fuck do we kill it? And notice I didn't say arrest it. Fuck that…"

"Okay, since it's just us, I'll tell you—I looked into buying silver bullets," said Doug.

"You shitting me?" asked Roy.

"Yeah, I'm shitting you. No silver bullets. No stakes or garlic or crosses. Just a nine millimeter hollow-point that I would love to use to remove this fucking thing's head."

"You remember that midget uptown? The Voo-Doo priest?" asked Roy.

"I am going to send you to sensitivity training, young man. Father Eduardo is vertically challenged, and he is an ordained Catholic priest."

"Yeah, right. Then you never met him."

"I did meet him. He actually was the one who convinced me that I wasn't totally off my rocker. I figured if a few million other people believe this stuff, I must not be so crazy after all."

"Well, I went to see him with Tim. And we asked him about killing this thing. Know what he said?"

Doug looked at him seriously. "No—what did he say?"

"He don't fuckin' know."

Doug threw his pizza on the paper plate. "Great. Then I'll stick to my original plan with my nine."

"And what do you do when you fire a full clip into him and he ain't dead?" whispered Roy, leaning in very close.

"I shit my pants and hope he finds me too disgusting to eat," said Doug with a small grin.

Roy chuckled. "Yeah, well, I want to go back and talk to the vertically challenged little dude with the bad-ass hat. Somebody out there in Voo-Doo Land must know how to kill this monster."

"Finish up and we'll take a ride," said Doug.

"I'm done—and don't think I didn't notice you putting tons of extra garlic on your pizza, you pussy."

Doug shrugged. "It's like chicken soup—it couldn't hurt."

Thirty-Three

Brodsky's

Adam had the afternoon to prepare himself for meeting Sara and her female friend. He made himself push away thoughts of eating them both, even though his lust for blood seemed insatiable these days. Adam thought for several hours about traveling with Sara, and in the end decided he would take a short trip with her out of the city. Maybe if he had a few days with her, to really spend time with her, he could convince her that she wanted to be just like him. It was a conversation that would be difficult to broach to say the least, but he would think of *something*.

It was early fall. Upstate New York would be beautiful this time of year. He'd find them a romantic place, secluded, but close enough to other humans lest he need to feed to avoid eating his companion. Adam decided that he would look into it. While he didn't own a computer himself, he did know of an internet café down the street. He would surf the net like a twenty-first century human and find a romantic getaway.

By late afternoon, Adam had located what looked like a very beautiful, upscale B & B in upstate New York. At almost seven hundred dollars a night, it would be enough to impress Sara. He smiled at the thoughts he was having. "Worrying about impressing a woman". It was so human. It was charming in a way, to actually care what someone thought or felt. He normally only worried about what they tasted like when he sucked their blood out of them. Adam was starting to believe that he actually felt the human emotion of "happiness", something he hadn't contemplated other than when associated with a meal.

Adam dressed in a nice pair of slacks, and even put on a tie and sport coat to meet Sara and her friend. He had considered feeding before he went, but had been overeating so much lately—he really had to keep that under control. The last thing he wanted was to have a bunch of policemen in New York City looking for him. Adam walked across town to meet Sara and her friend at the pub known as Brodsky's. He entered the crowded place. He was surprised at how many business people were rushing to a bar on a Monday right after work. He moved through the crowd, listening to the din of pumping hearts and boring conversations. He spotted Sara and an attractive woman about Sara's age standing by the tall bar.

Adam approached the pretty pair and smiled, and gave Sara a light kiss hello. He shook hands with Sharon as Sara introduced them.

"I've heard so much about you," said Sharon with a knowing grin. Apparently, Sara had bragged about Adam's special talents in bed—there was no mistaking Sara's slight blush.

"I hope it wasn't too bad," he said, in his most charming 'I-won't-eat-you' voice.

"Actually, I think Sara *likes you*, likes you!" she said with a laugh. "She won't shut up about you!"

Adam smiled. The girls had apparently had a cocktail or two already and were feeling a bit loose and silly. Sara was laughing at her friend, and play punched her arm with an exaggerated "*Shut up!*"

"Well, I like her very much, myself," said Adam, then put his arm around Sara's waist. He could feel her body heat and tried to ignore the urge to open her throat.

"Oh, *look* at you two already! It's disgusting!" joked Sharon.

"You're just *jealous*," said Sara with a dramatic toss of her thick hair. Adam smelled her shampoo and conditioner, and recalled lying on it.

"*Maybe…*" she replied, now playing sexy, and put her arms around Adam's waist to tease Sara. Adam smelled Sharon's liquor laced breath as she leaned in closer, but also something else. He breathed her in deeper and made a mental note of it.

They bantered back and forth for a while, and Adam easily won over Sara's friend, who was half convinced he must be wonderful before she ever met him. After an hour or so, Sharon excused herself, told Adam she was delighted to meet him, and left the bar to head home.

"She seems nice," he said. "She's a good friend?"

"My bestest buddy," said Sara. "You have any single guys for her? She needs a man like Adam Priest."

"Actually, she needs a doctor," said Adam softly.

"*What?*" she asked in surprise.

"Your friend," he said softly, remembering the smell of her breath. "She should see a doctor. Something wasn't quite right. If she's your friend, tell her to get a physical. Seriously."

Sara leaned away from him and made a face. "What are you *talking* about? Why would you *say* that?" She sounded annoyed.

"Don't get angry with me, Sara. I just have a knack with these things. You'll have to trust me. If I'm wrong, there's nothing lost other than a few minutes of her time. If I'm right, you can save her life."

Sara still looked pissed. "I don't think this is funny," she said.

"Either do I," he replied. "Tell her to see a doctor. If you doubt me, ask her if she has been having cramps lately. Especially in her lower right side. An appendix will burst if it gets too infected, and spill waste into the blood stream, poisoning the body and ruining the blood." It was an interesting choice of words.

"How could you tell by just looking at her?" asked Sara, now very concerned about his specific comment.

"I just can. Now…I need you to take off three days of work."

"Why?" she asked, still suspicious of her 'new boyfriend'.

"I want to take you out of the city, to a very beautiful B&B up on a lake, in beautiful mountains, and see the fall foliage." (He flashed back to old Prussia for a moment and remembered the beautiful mountains with their ancient forests.)

"Really?" she asked in genuine shock. "I mean, just like that? We take off for three days and go to the mountains?"

"Just like that. It's a beautiful place. At least, it looked like it on the computer. It's an exclusive place. Several hundred acres of woodlands and a huge lake. I think it would be nice to get out of this city for a while, and get to know you a little better." He leaned in and kissed her, and she kissed him back, still in minor shock. It had been an interesting five minutes.

"I'm not sure if I can take the time off of work right now—it's so busy. I mean, it sounds wonderful, really, thank you so much for even thinking of it, but can it wait for the weekend? We could go Friday to Sunday? I could probably take off Friday."

Adam sighed. He had forgotten about 'work'. He hadn't worked, other than as a soldier, for decades. And even during those days, he found it more 'interesting' than actual work. Physical labor was nothing to him. As long as he had access to food, he could tolerate any conditions. The past thirty years had been his laziest. He lived in a nice apartment, ate whenever he wanted, and had access to everything that a city like New York offered to stay entertained, should he get bored with his existence. Maybe that's where Sara fit in—it ended boredom?

"Okay, Sara. Friday then. We'll leave Friday morning and head upstate. Just a few hours away, but it will feel like another world." Adam thought about his world was so different than hers. Would she come willingly to his?

They chatted about all kinds of things for another hour or so, and then Sara wanted to leave. "She had to work tomorrow", and didn't want to drink too much or stay out too late. She invited Adam back home with her, and he paused only for a moment. Could he control himself? He hadn't fed in two days now. She smelled so good. Her heartbeat was so strong. He could almost feel her exploding into his mouth, the hot arterial spray. He could control it, he told himself. He wanted to be with her again and see her without her clothes on. He wanted to experience physical closeness with her again. It was so human—and so warm. He smiled and whispered, "Let's go…"

Thirty-Four

Father Eduardo

Roy and Doug drove up town through crazy Manhattan mid-day Monday traffic. Taxis honked and swerved through each other in a game of kamikaze-kabby, cursing at each other as they accelerated, only to brake again a moment later. They parked illegally in front of the brightly colored church and walked up the stairs. A few mothers sat on the steps watching pre-schoolers jump rope out front. They entered the church and found father Eduardo standing on a bench, speaking to a member of his church. He recognized the two of them and pointed towards his office, and they walked back to the same office they had originally met him in while he finished his conversation with the parishioner.

The pair sat in the small office until Eduardo appeared, in his strange attire and leather cap. They stood when he walked in and the priest motioned for them to sit, then used a small stepstool to climb up into a leather chair.

"De last time I saw *you*," he said, pointing to Roy, "You were with a large police officer. And you, you worked alone—FBI, is it?"

Doug nodded. "Yes, Father Eduardo. It was about a year ago."

"So now da' two of you are working together looking for 'dis monster that lives among us?"

"Yes, sir, you could say that," said Roy.

"And what about your partner from before? He is well, I take it?"

"Heart attack, actually. But he'll be okay," said Roy.

"Heart attack. Dey got cures for 'dat. Being eaten alive—ain't got no cure for 'dat."

Roy cleared his throat. "Yeah. Well…listen, Father, we came back because we have some more questions. And we don't want to appear, um, *unprofessional*, you know what I mean? But…"

"But you are starting to believe de impossible now, ain't dat' da truth of da' whole t'ing?" said the little man, now leaning over intensely.

"Well, we don't '*not* believe it'—how's that? Can we just say, for the sake of argument, that what we are trying to find *is* some type of evil creature that isn't quite human. Let's say, purely for the sake of argument, that it *was* one of the mythical creatures from one of your old books. How would we destroy it? Can we just shoot it?"

Father Eduardo sat back, the chair looking like a huge throne against his small physique, his leather cap, a crown of sorts.

"In de bible, der' are stories and references to t'ings. Matthew and Ezekiel both wrote about t'ings dat' maybe we'd call zombies or undead creatures. And who knows how many t'ings dey' wrote dat' were lost over de' ages?"

"With all due respect, I don't recall Dracula being in the bible, Father," said Roy.

"Ezekiel 37:1-14!" said Eduardo looking serious. "He describes de bones of de dead comin' together and re-animating. And Matthew, 27:52-53, describes de resurrection of de dead. Maybe in de ancient days, a man came out of a coma, and dey thought he returned from de dead? Or maybe dey saw somet'ing else? Or maybe it was never human to begin wit. Maybe dey didn't see no Dracula like de movies, but maybe dey saw some t'ing we would never believe widout us seein' it first."

Roy recalled their conversation about dinosaurs. Who would believe those stories without seeing the bones?

Doug spoke softly. "I have a friend who is a Scuba Diver. He keeps a huge reef tank in his house. One day I saw this thing called a Medusa Worm moving across the sand. It was red. Looked like two feet of intestines with a mouth at one end that had ten fern-like appendages sticking out of it. It kept the tank clean for him—a detritus eater. If the thing was a land animal, and a little bigger, no one would ever leave their home. Scariest and strangest thing I ever saw. Point is, there's a lot of stuff out there in the world that is hard to explain or understand. And personally, Father, I don't need to explain it *or* understand it. I just want to know how to kill it."

Roy added, "Will bullets kill it? I mean, in the books you have—how did the villagers kill these things?"

Father Eduardo tapped his pudgy fingertips together. "After de very first time I spoke wit you, Mr. FBI Man, I went back and looked at dem books again. I read enough stories to give myself nightmares. *Nightmares.* And not in one of dem stories did I read about any of de people killing dis t'ing. In one book, dere were pictures of de t'ings head up on a pole. So dey managed to kill it. Maybe dey cut off it's head. I don't know."

"In the Vampire movies, they use crosses and garlic and stakes through the heart. Think any of that stuff is based on old folk lore for a reason?" asked Roy, thinking back to the garlic of Doug's pizza.

Father Eduardo shrugged. "I always have to assume dat stories are based on somet'ing in reality. It's how Christianity works, ain't dat right? A man is de son of God and dies for us, and comes back to life. Is dat just a story? Or did it happen wit so many people knowing it was da truth dat the story survives to *dis* day?" Father Eduardo hopped off his chair and walked back and forth in his office, pacing and speaking like he was preaching. "Do da monsters in our stories come from a survival instinct in some deep part of de brain, or do we all believe dese stories because we know dat it's true? And for every scary story, didn't momma and poppa have de solution? De werewolf can be killed by a silver bullet. De vampire by a stake tru de heart. A witch gets melted by water. Momma and poppa always had to have a way to put de baby back to sleep, right? Always a cure for de curse."

"So you're saying you believe there's always a way to kill these things, no matter what it is?" asked Roy.

"No. I'm sayin momma and poppa *made up* a ting so de baby can be put back to sleep. But maybe dey just made it up. Maybe de idea dat everyt'ing out dere can be killed by humans is just a lie to keep us all from dyin' of fright."

"Thanks, that's very reassuring," said Roy quietly.

Doug shook his head. "You were supposed to be helping us," he said quietly.

"I can only help wit what I know. I know dis much. Der is too much out der in der world dat can't be explained. Like da t'ing in the fishtank. It just wanna eat, right? Ugly scary t'ing that just wanna feed and survive. And maybe make more baby t'ings like hisself."

"That's a scary thought," said Roy.

"Yeah, mon. Eat and make babies. Dat everyt'ing on dis planet."

"Except priests," said Roy, throwing a barb at him.

Eduardo smiled, showing his gold teeth. "So. Maybe now you believe in t'ings you don't understand. Maybe you believe in what you don't see. Maybe now you ready to lift it up to God?"

"Excuse me?" asked Roy.

"Time you ask God to help you. Maybe he send you an angel like Michael to kill dis t'ing."

"He sent me a nine millimeter," said Doug. "And Roy. He sent me Roy. And me and Roy are gonna' shoot this thing whatever it is, and if I need to cut its head off to kill it, then that's what we'll do."

Father Eduardo walked over and patted Doug's leg. "Dat get a hallelujah!"

Roy pondered and then spoke. "Father, from what you have read, are there any descriptions of the thing? I mean, are we looking for something that looks like a human?"

"You ever read Milton? John Milton—'Paradise Lost'?" asked the priest.

"Um, no—I must have been sick that day at school," said Roy, embarrassed that he recognized the name, but nothing else about the epic poem of good and evil.

"Well, in dat story, my favorite t'ing to read outside de bible, it is de devil dat gets all de good lines. De smooth talker—de stylin groove— dat's Satin. De angels, dey square. Boring. It's de devil that speaks so sweet and convincing. I believe evil don't have to *look* evil to *be* evil. Maybe dis t'ing look just like you. Or you."

"Or you," said Roy, smiling.

Eduardo belly laughed. "Yeah, mon. Maybe he handsome like me. But to your question…I don't t'ink you look at him and know. Not unless you catch him eating."

"Yeah, watching a person rip open someone's arteries and suck their blood out might give us a clue," said Roy.

"So we have to catch him in the act?" pondered Doug. "We'll have to try and find times of death on all these cases. I don't seem to recall him only feeding at midnight or full moons and or anything like that."

"Dat's for you detectives to figure out. But you figure it out, and you find it, and you kill it and cut off its evil head. Den we all sleep better at night." Father Eduardo climbed back up into his chair, and Doug and Roy thanked him for his time.

Thirty-Five

Adam & Sara

Adam didn't see Sara Tuesday or Wednesday, although he spoke to her several times on the phone after Monday night's sexual activities. He could feel his desire for blood coming on stronger and knew he'd need to feed soon. He also knew he had been getting careless and was being a glutton. Over the years, there had been a few narrow escapes from villagers and police in various countries. While he didn't feel scared and didn't understand the concept of worry, he didn't like inconvenience. Being forced to move all the time was inconvenient. He liked his current situation—the apartment, the clothes and Goth Girl's fur coat, the city. He wanted to be able to stay even after Sara joined him in his existence. He decided to "go out" for dinner.

Thursday night, Adam took the PATH train into Newark. He was dressed in shoddy clothes and tried his best to blend in to the crowd heading back across the Hudson in the evenings commute. When he arrived in Newark, Adam left the station and began walking. The rebuilt part of Newark around the train station wasn't too bad, but as he walked further away from it, the neighborhoods grew seedier. He kept walking until it began to get dark. He left the residential areas and meandered into sleazy commercial areas with abandoned buildings and dirty sweatshops. Sweatshops had been, for over a hundred years, a great source of food. The migrant workers could be easily found, eaten, and never investigated. Most of them feared the police, and when a co-worker disappeared, no one other than the family noticed.

Adam found a factory that was busy manufacturing clothes, filled with illegal aliens working for seven dollars an hour six days a week, and waited. Shift change ended up being at eleven, and Adam watched the street fill up with weary factory workers. Most would be walking home to save bus fare, and the streets of Newark were dark. Adam had decided he would gorge himself this evening to try and satiate, even temporarily, his lust for Sara's blood. He needed enough to last for a few days out the city. He walked far that night, following a group of Spanish speaking men and women for almost a mile and a half into darker, dingier parts of the city. When they came to a quieter part of the city, where few cars drove by so late, and the street lights were all broken and not replaced, he pounced. Three women and two men. The largest meal in a very long time. He wounded them all enough to incapacitate them without killing them, then dragged them behind an old house.

It took him almost three hours to finish all of them in an orgiastic shower of blood and human tissue. The ecstasy was indescribable. He dragged them inside the old boarded up house, one at a time, and arranged them in what had been a den. He built a bonfire in the center of the room, like the group had been seated around the fire, and lit the place up. Adam pulled off his blood soaked jacket and shoved it into the fire. The old building burned even faster than he anticipated, and by the time he was a few blocks away, the fire was through the roof, and the house was collapsing. It reminded Adam of the farmhouse he had burned over a century before, when he tasted his first female victim. Reminiscing near the crackling of the fire brought his mind back to Sara, which made him smile and think about making her his companion for eternity.

Although it was cold out and Adam didn't have his jacket, he was very warm with so much blood filling his body. Adam burped and smiled.

"Such a pig," he said out loud to no one in particular. He spit out a tiny piece of flesh stuck between his teeth. He hadn't gorged like this in so long; the feeling was no less than total euphoria.

By the time Adam arrived home, it was almost two in the morning. His cell phone sat on the counter with several voicemails from Sara. He smiled as he listened to her apologetic, slightly hysterical voice.

"Adam, it's Sara. I have been trying to reach you—I'm at the hospital with Sharon. She called me and told me she wasn't feeling well and I told her to get to the ER immediately. I felt like an idiot in case I was over-reacting, but what you said at the bar...oh my God, Adam. Her appendix burst. If she hadn't gotten there when she did, she might have died. You saved her life, Adam. I don't know how you knew, but you did. She was fighting with me about going to the doctor and I made her go to the ER because of you! And you saved her! I don't know what to say. I hardly know you, but I swear, I think I love you already. Thank you, Adam! Call me on my cell when you get this."

Adam smiled. He had smelled the toxins in Sharon's blood. Her appendix was already leaking very slightly, and eating her would have tasted foul. She would live. Sara would love him. She would want to be like him. Forever.

Thirty-Six

Following the Bloody Trail

It was early Friday morning, and Roy was fast asleep. He had been working crazy hours on his investigation. The LT and Captain Ammiano had gotten busy with other cases, and his "taskforce" now consisted of occasional phone calls to Heather Connell and his new "partner" Agent Patmore. It wasn't that Captain Ammiano or Lieutenant Alexander weren't interested in the case, they were—but they also knew that the Sixth had several officers from the task force still working on it full time, and with Roy working with Doug, they felt like they were contributing as much as they could. New York was a busy city. The captain was perpetually buried in paperwork, and the lieutenant was responsible for managing five other sergeants. Captain Alexander told Roy to work as much overtime as he wanted, and to "take the ball and run with it" with Doug Patmore.

On the third ring, Roy mumbled a groggy "hello".

"Hey, Pisano," said a horse voice.

"Holy shit, I thought you were dead," said Roy, starting to smile at Tim's voice.

"Nah, I just feel that way. They finally hooked up my phone. I woulda' called and woke your ass up hours ago. I can't believe you're sleeping and not tracking our psycho."

Roy sat up and flipped on his bedside lamp. "How you feeling, Tim? No shit—how are ya?"

"The doughnuts you sent were delicious. You sadistic bastard. I had to watch the nurses chew them from the other side of the window. That's fuckin' *cold*, Pisano."

Roy laughed. It was good to hear Tim's voice.

"I'm doing okay I guess. They cracked open my chest. It's like having diarrhea—you're afraid to cough, know what I mean?"

"Wear brown pajamas."

"No, it's not that—I'm afraid I'll shoot my heart and lungs across the room. Besides, all I have on is a very large green gown that is open in the back. Paints a pretty picture, huh?"

"Jesus. And I just woke up. And hey, listen, if you *do* blow your organs across the room, I know a guy that would love to eat them."

"Don't make me laugh, you sick fuck. Oh man, that hurts."

"That's what you get for calling me so early on my day off."

"Any progress?" asked Tim, now in a quieter, more serious tone.

"Well, Doug and I went back to see the witch doctor. I swear, Tim, that little fucker gives me nightmares every time I talk to him. Anyway, just between us..." he stopped. How do you even say it out loud?

"Yeah?"

"Man, it's fucked up."

"No shit. Now tell me what's going on. Whatcha' got?"

"All right—and just listen. Doug and I have been cross referencing cases on missing persons, dead bodies that went unsolved, unsolved rape-murders…"

"He's raping them now, too? Jesus…"

"Just *listen*! This fucking creature, and I do mean creature, has been killing and eating victims for a few *decades*, Tim. He ingests the DNA of a victim, goes on to his next, and occasionally leaves us *that* DNA at his next victim. It's like a game of pass the DNA. We've been working backwards all week. If I didn't see it I wouldn't believe it. It's not too easy to comprehend."

"Can I talk now?" asked Tim.

"Yeah."

"That's fucked up, Pisano."

Roy grunted a "No shit."

"That's really the angle you're working? That this guy is really some kind of monster that literally ingests blood and DNA, eats people, rapes women, and goes on doing this for *decades* without getting caught? You fucking with me, Roy? I'm on morphine, but I think I am following you."

"You're following me, Tim. I know. It's unbelievable. But we have bite marks that span like sixty years, DNA from thirty plus years, and an overlap of cross referenced cases that only make sense when you accept that it's one guy that is a fucking vampire or some shit. *I know. I know…*"

"I'm kind of glad I'm in here on morphine. Otherwise you would have given me a wicked headache. Seriously, Roy, you believe what you just told me?"

"Tim—Doug and I talked a long time. Here's what we have come up with. We don't have to *understand* it—we don't even have to *believe* it—we just have to use the evidence to catch up with this thing and *kill* it."

"And that Fed believes it, too—the whole thing. Vampires?"

"Yeah. And you remember Father Eduardo. When you listen to him and see the evidence, it's hard *not* to believe it. It's like, we don't *have* to understand it, but if we give in to the *possibility*, then maybe we solve the case. When we try a rational approach, nothing fits. When we accept this crazy vampire shit, it all makes *total* sense."

"Roy, I'm gonna' hang up now and sleep for a couple of hours. Then I'm going to call you back and see if we had this conversation or if I dreamed the whole thing."

"Come on, Tim—you were almost there yourself before you had your heart attack."

Tim sighed heavily. "Roy, I *was* there. And I think that's what gave me the fucking heart attack. Good luck, Pisano. I'm sorry to bail on you."

Thirty-Seven

A little getaway

Friday morning, Adam walked down to his lobby to wait for Sara. Unlike him, she owned a car, something many city dwellers didn't bother with because parking was so expensive. She pulled up and he walked out wearing blue jeans and a turtleneck under a flannel shirt, trying his best to look like every lumberjack picture he had ever seen. Sara was smiling broadly when he hopped into her little car and kissed her hello.

"Look at you!" she said with a laugh. "I had no idea you were such the outdoorsman!"

"And good morning to you," he said. His color was excellent, and his eyes were deep blue. He felt like he was burning up under his ridiculous costume. The blood of five hard working immigrants was pumping hard in his beating heart.

"So where are we going?" she asked with excitement in her voice. "I have a GPS. If you give me the address, I can just follow the directions off of here."

Adam handed her the directions and informational pamphlet he had printed out about the B&B.

"Oh my *God*, Adam! This place looks *amazing*! Look at the stone fireplace! Look at that *Jacuzzi*!" She leaned over and gave him a better kiss. "We are going to have a great weekend."

"I'm sure we'll never forget it," he said with a smile.

Sara pulled away from the curb and drove across town, following her GPS out of the city. She updated Adam about Sharon, and thanked him a dozen times for saving her life. She pressed him about "how he knew", but he gave vague answers and changed topics expertly, and she was excited enough about their road trip that she eventually let it go for the time being. She did call Sharon to check on her, and Adam smiled as he listened to Sara describe the B&B to her friend. She was squealing like a little kid on Christmas morning, and Adam found her excitement encouraging. To listen to Sara describe the small resort to her friend, one would have thought Adam was taking her to Paris for the weekend. Even Sharon, who was still feeling like she had been hit by a bus, was smiling on her end of the phone. She reminded Sara to thank Adam for her a dozen times, and Sara promised she would call and check on her soon.

They drove for three and a half hours, deep into the Adirondack Mountains where the leaves were already burning red, orange and yellow. It was spectacular, and the weather report had promised crisp, clear autumn days, and frosty nights in front of the fire. The smell of the leaves and pines was strong, even inside the car. Adam inhaled it deeply, his mind racing back through time to the woods of Jena. How appropriate that Sara would enter her new life after death in such a similar setting as her creator. Tiny little towns came and went as they drove the winding mountain roads to their destination—a lavish Bed& Breakfast "resort" called Tall Pines. It had been given the coveted Five Diamonds Award in the "Best of the Best" travel guide, and as they pulled in to the small village of chalet-looking cottages, they could see why.

A bellhop, dressed in a long green tuxedo coat and top, greeted them as they pulled in, and opened their doors with white gloves. He formally welcomed them and brought them inside to "the house" as he called it, where an older man smiled and immediately offered them a choice of coffee, regular or "Irish", wine, spirits...whatever they wanted. He informed them that lunch would be served in the house from noon to three, or it could be brought to their chalet.

Sara hung on every word, and Adam smiled at her excitement. He had traveled all over the world—very little impressed him anymore, but he could see that Sara was not used to the five-diamond treatment. The bellman escorted them personally down a pebble path to their A-Frame styled chalet. Adam smiled at the ridiculous architecture that tried to mimic Tudor, Swiss Chalet, and log cabin all in one structure. It even had stained glass windows. Ludicrous.

"Oh my God, Adam! It's amazing!"

"Yes, it *is* beautiful, isn't it?" he lied. "It looks straight out of a Swiss Village." (Or Disneyland, he thought.)

The bellman brought in their bags and Adam gave him a nice tip and told him to return with his best bottle of French red as soon as possible.

After he left, Sara pounced on Adam and gave him a big hug and kiss. "You don't have to get me drunk to get my clothes off," she said, unbuttoning his flannel shirt.

Adam smiled at her excitement. She was beaming and he could feel her heart beating faster as she unbuttoned her shirt. "Are you sure you want to do that already?" he asked. "You don't want to walk around and see this place first?"

She ignored him and took his shirt off as fast as she could. He allowed her to pull his turtleneck off over his head as he kicked off his shoes. She was on her knees in front of Adam when the knock came at the front door. "Oh shit!" Sara exclaimed, blushing while still kneeling in front of Adam. She looked at him, quite naked and hard, and said, "I better answer the door! Go hide in the bathroom!" Sara was still clothed, and she was laughing at being "busted" by the bellman. Adam walked to the bathroom, quite calmly. It would take more than being interrupted while having sex with a willing female to fluster *him*. "Hurry up!" she yelled after him while she straightened out her clothes and opened the door slightly. The bellman didn't crack a smile, even though he saw her lipstick thoroughly smeared across her mouth and chin and noticed the obvious difference in the state of her hair where Adam had been holding it.

He handed her the bottle through the door and asked if she would like to have him uncork it for them. This wasn't the first time he had showed up at the wrong time in the quiet resort, and he knew how to be tactful. When she said she'd open it later, he told her the corkscrew was by the wine glasses on the back bar. Sara thanked him and took the bottle, pulled a crumpled up five dollar bill from her jeans, and sent him on his way. She locked the door behind him, pulled off her own clothes and ran to the bathroom where Adam was sitting by the Jacuzzi. She walked in naked, holding up the bottle, and asked, "Which would you rather have first?"

Thirty-Eight

FBI New York Office – Pistol Range

Doug had picked up Roy from his apartment and drove him downtown to the Federal Plaza main office. As they drove downtown, Roy asked where they were going.

"Main office for some stress relief," said Doug. "I'm taking you to the pistol range."

"You find shooting relaxing?" asked Roy.

"No. What I find relaxing is knowing my partner can hit the target every time he fires," he said without a smile.

They joked around a bit and talked about the investigation, parked in the garage under the office, and took a secured elevator up to the range.

"You weren't kidding," said Roy as they walked to the range and signed in with the range officer.

"I don't kid about this. I qualify every three months. When was the last time you did?"

"We qualify every year," said Roy quietly.

"Once. You want to go a dollar a point?" asked Doug.

Roy was a pretty good shot, and had received the expert marksman badge most years when he qualified, but he wasn't going to get suckered in by a Fed. He ignored him. They walked to the range, said a few hellos, and Doug set Roy up with glasses and ear protection, then dialed up the targets. The target of a man's silhouette moved down the range to fifty feet away and stopped.

Doug told Roy to go first. Roy leveled his Glock 17 nine millimeter pistol and closed one eye. He had seventeen rounds in his weapon and slowly began squeezing off the trigger. He emptied his gun, yelled "clear", and Doug pressed a button that retrieved the paper target. He quickly counted the holes.

"Fifteen rounds in the coke bottle, three in the heart. Not bad," said Doug. The "coke bottle" was the center part of the silhouette shaped like the namesake. In the center of *that* was a six-inch round circle where the heart was located. Roy had hit inside the target's coke-bottle fifteen times, and of those, three were "heart shots". Two bullets had missed the target completely, but overall, it was very good shooting for most cops.

Doug hooked up a new target and sent it down the same fifty feet. He picked up his weapon and squeezed off the same seventeen rounds, a bit faster. He retrieved his target. Roy couldn't help but mutter a "holy shit". Fifteen head shots, two in the throat.

"Practice makes perfect," said Doug. "I usually hit all seventeen."

"You don't count the two in the throat?"

"Only headshots. No fucking around," he said softly. "Let's go again at a hundred feet, then a few mags at close quarters."

Doug and Roy spent almost an hour in the range, and Roy was amazed at Doug's accuracy. When they were finished, they checked out with the range officer and Doug signed his targets and stuffed them in an envelope for the Range Master to document. While it wasn't an "official" qualification round, it would still go in Doug's records.

"Jesus, man. I thought I was a good shot. That was embarrassing," said Roy as they walked out.

"We train a little more than you do," said Doug. "And we train for headshots."

"Don't fuck with the FBI," said Roy.

"Exactly. Even if you are an undead, bloodsucking, vampire. I plan on emptying my full magazine into that thing's head one of these days real soon," said Doug. "I am relieved to know you will at least be hitting the thing with me."

They drove back uptown to Doug's small office in the unidentified FBI substation and started pulling out files again. They now had almost two hundred cases that overlapped with DNA or other trace evidence, linking unrelated people through a seemingly impossible thread of common evidence. Once the "handoff theory" of DNA being passed along through the various cases was accepted as believable, the string of vicious murders and mutilations could be traced back almost sixty years with startling similarities.

Roy leaned back in his chair with his fingers interlaced on top of his head and started thinking out loud. "Okay, Doug. So let's say this is all the same killer. How can we use what we have to try and get *ahead* of him? The times of day, the days of the week, the intervals between these cases—everything is different. Except for the trail of DNA from case to case, we don't have shit. And we have huge gaps in our timeline, I'm sure. For every case we have here that we can link to this thing, how many are we missing?"

Doug rubbed his tired eyes. "I think about that all the time. How many have we missed? How many other victims are out there? This is the strangest case I have ever worked, and not just by a little. And to answer your question, I don't know how to get ahead of him yet. We need to keep trying to get some names for him. Aliases, anything. The print that we found at Goth Girl's apartment matched another murder, but it was never solved, so there's no ID there. I'm stumped, too, Roy."

"Let's get inside his head," said Roy.

"I tried that for twenty months. I had the best shrinks in the FBI doing profiles for me, and they are all over the place. I have no less than seven profiles for this guy, and they are all totally different, because none of the shrinks would ever accept the idea that we're dealing with something non-human."

"You told them it was non-human?"

"Hell, no. I like my job in the Bureau. But their theories on the type of person that would do this are all a waste of time. This guy is not like any serial killer we've ever seen, because he isn't necessarily killing them in his mind—he's merely feeding."

Roy leaned forward. "Okay—so let's work it that way. He's not a killer for the sake of killing—he's merely feeding. So you're him, and you need to eat human blood. What would do for a job? Where would you live? How would you pick victims?"

Doug pulled out a notebook that was filled with his notes. "Roy, I've got a book full of those questions to myself with my theories. Where would you live? You'd live in New York City with seven million people in close quarters that wouldn't miss a few stragglers. How would you pick victims? The way he's been doing it is smart. He picks people who can go missing easily. Hookers, homeless people, anyone who isn't easily noticed. Maybe he's smart enough to grab up illegals from non-English speaking communities who are afraid of the police."

"What about a job? The guy needs money."

"I thought about that, too. I figure he pulls enough cash off his victims that he can survive on that. Maybe not live rich, but get by. If he's not picky, there are plenty of cheap places to live in the city's poor neighborhoods."

"You think he'd maybe work at a blood bank? A hospital? Access to blood that way?"

"I thought about that, too. I checked his prints against every hospital and medical center that requires them in the city. Nothing."

"So *now* what?"

"We keep working the cases and hope we get lucky. We just need a little break…"

Thirty-Nine

Adirondacks

Adam and Sara made love like Honeymooners the entire first afternoon. Adam insisted on a picnic rather than eating in bed, since it would be impossible to hide "not eating" while lying naked in bed with Sara. The chef at the house prepared a nice meal and bagged it for them, and Adam and Sara went hiking up the trails into the mountains. Sara had brought her camera and was enthralled with the landscapes. She snapped a few shots of Adam, but his eyes kept coming out funny and she was getting frustrated with her photography abilities, blaming herself for the way his blue eyes looked silver in the color pictures or totally black in the black and white the pictures. She cursed her camera, and Adam encouraged her to concentrate on the scenery and wildlife instead.

Sara snapped away—frogs, birds, foliage, mountainscapes, trees… it was beautiful, although a bit cold in the mountains. Adam enjoyed watching her. She loved the details of nature, and her passion for trying to capture it on film led him to start his line of questions that he hoped would ultimately lead to the conversation he wanted to have with her. He spoke philosophically as they walked, hoping to capture her deepest thoughts on life and death and afterlife. Or was it afterdeath?

"It's amazing, isn't it, Sara? The interconnection of everything. The whole life cycle is so visible out here."

"It really is. I *love* fall. Everything dies so boldly! The colors *screaming*, like a protest against their death. Then bleak winter—then the spring brings it all back again. I *love* the change of seasons."

Adam loved what she had said. "*Yes*, the colors *screaming* in protest of their death. I wouldn't have imagined you seeing it that way. But it really *is* like that, isn't it?"

Sara smiled. "Well, no one wants to die, not even the leaves. Survival instinct." She knelt down and snapped a black and white picture of a fern against a stone background. It was perhaps clichéd, but beautiful nonetheless.

Adam was smiling again at her comment. She understood perhaps more than he had given her credit for. "Yes, survival instinct. You can pull the legs off of a frog and it will refuse to die. It won't lie down and just roll over. In fact, it may even regenerate a leg."

"Well, that's gross, but I see your point."

Adam frowned. "Nature is *vicious*, Sara. This serene scene before you. Do you think it is all love and peace out here?"

"It's *beautiful* out here!" she said with a smile, and snapped another picture of him. "Damn! You eyes are so blue they won't come out right!"

"You are naïve, pretty girl. The roots of these quiet trees run underground and try and kill their competitors. The weeds and flowers send poisonous chemicals underground to murder each other. They make poison from their leaves and berries. Birds eat every insect they can find. Insects with stingers, by the way, that would poison and eat their prey as well."

She looked at him with a funny expression. "Why the dark mood? It's so nice out here. Why are thinking about all the violence and death. You just got laid for three hours! You should be in a *great* mood!" She stood up and gave him a quick kiss.

"I *am* in a great mood. And I can still taste you," he said, trying not to picture her throat ripped open. "It's just that I want to know more about you. About how you perceive the world. Life and death."

"Holy cow, Adam. Most guys roll over and go to sleep after sex. You get *deep!*" She laughed. "Life and death, huh? I have no idea, really. I'm a good Catholic girl, although I guess you wouldn't know after today's session, huh?" She blushed slightly. "I guess I believe in Heaven. I figure, *eventually*, we will all find out. In the spring, everything comes back to life. Maybe that's what happens to us, too."

Adam smiled. "There's something 'after'. I'm *quite* sure."

"I never asked you, are you religious? What *are* you?"

"I am the reverse of religious. Those that would offer an opinion on afterlife have no *clue* about that which they preach. The churches are a joke. A business. Their talk of God is angering, like *they* know something *we* don't."

Sara was surprised by his angry tone. "So you're an *atheist*? Agnostic? What turned you off?"

"A lifetime of experience. A very long lifetime. I believe in what I see out here—the frogs eating the bugs. The birds eating the frogs. The snakes eating the birds. The need to feed and survive. It's a vicious world, Sara. There is predator and prey. That's all."

"Well, you *did* eat me earlier,' she joked, trying to lighten his mood.

He didn't smile, thinking about what it would be like to eat her heart and liver. To suck her body dry of every last drop of blood and watch the life drain out of her.

"Come on, Adam! I'm joking! You have a *dark* side," she said with her pleasant laugh.

"You have no idea," he said. He forced himself to smile and lighten things up a bit, but he wasn't done pursing his conversation with her. He kissed her, and took her by the hand, leading further up the trail. It was steep and she was breathing heavier, the noise of her breathing making Adam crazy inside. He wanted to hear her scream in pain…he pushed the thoughts away.

"So if you don't believe in God, what's the meaning of life? Everything just eats everything it can?" Sara was playing with him.

"Everything eats and reproduces," he said, thinking about the dog he had to tear apart in his apartment after creating its new life after death. Or was it death after life?

"Eats, reproduces and dies," she said.

"Not always," he said.

Sara laughed. "So you *do* believe in Heaven!"

"I didn't say that. I just know there is more than what you see."

"And how do you know?" asked Sara, intrigued by this interesting man who treated her so well, was wonderful in bed (and on the counter and in the Jacuzzi and against the wall), and had a very serious side that she was now seeing for the first time.

"I have seen things you can't even imagine," Adam said softly as they walked along the trail.

She looked over at him, a bit uneasy at his tone. "You mean, like in the army?"

"Oh yes, there, too. Unimaginable suffering. So much *blood*, Sara. Blood is life. It's what it's all about I suppose. Blood. The life force. I've seen it leave so many humans. You watch the eyes go dim. The heart stops it loud pounding." He could hear *her* heart beating faster from the uphill walk. "The screaming. People torn to pieces."

Sara was now feeling uncomfortable. "I'm so sorry, Adam. I had no idea about your life in the army. I guess you had some horrible experiences."

"Horrible? No. I wouldn't say horrible. I would say it was life changing," he said with a smile that gave her goose bumps, his silvery blue eyes now lost in a sea of time as he remembered Jena.

Forty

Saturday in the City

oy and Doug were back at Doug's office when Roy's cell phone rang. It was captain Ammiano. Doug watched his very animated cop partner on the phone with his boss. Roy was talking a hundred miles an hour and scribbling down notes. He was making gestures to Doug as he spoke, letting Doug know that something huge was going on. When he finished, he thanked the captain and screamed at Doug.

"We got that son of a bitch! Finally! We got something!"

Doug stood up without even realizing it. "What? What have you got?"

"Last night in Jersey, three women and two men were killed in a house fire. By coincidence, these same five illegals were working in a sweatshop in Newark. The shirt factory had video surveillance. Make a long story short—the five workers went missing. Some of their family and friends checked with their boss. Then they got the news about the fire in some abandoned house—but these people didn't *live* at that address! Somebody killed them and put them there, and then torched the place to cover it up—sound familiar?"

"They got a picture of our guy?"

"Yes! The shirt factory went back through last night's tapes to see what time they left, if they were together, all the usual questions for the Newark cops. In the video, there is a guy standing around outside for a long time watching the joint, and then he follows this group of workers as they leave. The motherfucker looked *right* into the camera! Captain Ammiano is emailing it us right now! Open your email!"

Doug hopped into his seat and punched up his mail, saw the document with attached photo and opened it on his screen. It was a black and white photo, and a bit dark and grainy, but you could definitely see the man's face clear enough to make an ID. "Son of a bitch," he whispered without even realizing he was speaking out loud. He was looking into the face of pure evil.

"That's it? *That's* our vampire?" asked Roy, somewhat amazed that the thing looked like a regular man, about thirty years old.

"Weird, huh?" asked Doug. "I'm not sure what I was expecting, but I guess it wasn't this guy. Then again, serial killers were always the quiet guy that lived next door, too, know what I mean?"

"Let's get this face on every television set in America! *Someone* out there knows who the fuck this sick bastard is!" screamed Roy, his adrenaline pumping like a linebacker before the big play.

"Doing it right now. I'm emailing my boss, too. This is the first real break in almost two years of busting my ass, Roy. This is huge!"

"Damn right. Pure luck. We had notified every department in the five boroughs and in north Jersey and southern Connecticut about this guy's MO. Any mysterious deaths, arsons, violent murders, dead bodies—anything and everything was to be sent to the task force. Captain Ammiano saw it and checked with Newark. That video tape may have just broken this wide open."

Within two hours, every news network in the tri-state area was broadcasting pictures of a man wanted for questioning in several violent crimes. While he wasn't listed as a suspect, he was listed as a subject of interest that should not be approached, but should be reported to authorities immediately. A phone number for the FBI's special switchboard set up a dedicated call center and waited. It didn't take long.

. . .

SHARON WHITE HAD BEEN HALF dozing in her hospital room, heavily sedated after her emergency appendectomy. She was sore and tired, and had to blink three or four times to make sure she wasn't hallucinating when she saw Adam's face on the television. She listened to the broadcast and grew terrified. There was *no* doubt—this was the same man Sara had introduced to her at the pub. The same guy that saved her life by making Sara tell her to go to the hospital. She grabbed the phone and dialed the number on the television screen. She was transferred twice after telling her story, thanked for calling in, and transferred yet again. When the call was sent directly to Doug's office, he put her on speaker phone and he and Roy took the call themselves.

"Miss White? This is Special Agent Doug Patmore with the FBI. I am sitting here with Sergeant Roy Ruiz of the NYPD and this call is being taped. Thank you for calling. Can you please tell us everything you know about the subject in the picture?"

"As I told the other woman…"

"Please just start from the very beginning," said Doug calmly. "Go back as far as you can, and give us every detail."

"I was with my best friend Sara. She introduced me to her boyfriend. His name is Adam Priest…"

She continued to speak as Roy hopped behind Doug's desk and accessed the New York Police Department's CODIS computer. Within a few seconds, he had twenty seven Adam Priests living in Manhattan. He pulled up all of the driver's licenses and went photo to photo until he saw the same man from the video surveillance staring back at him from Doug's screen. He grabbed Doug's arm as Doug scribbled notes from Sharon. Doug nodded as he looked at the screen, and continued his questioning. He took Sharon off speaker phone so Roy could talk to him without Sharon hearing him.

Doug asked Sharon, "And he told Sara that you needed a doctor?"

"*Yes*! He saved my life! I don't think he is any *killer*, officer. But the report I saw on TV scared me. He and Sara went away together this weekend. If he is some type of dangerous criminal, Sara needs to know right away."

"Have you attempted to call her yet?" asked Doug, now very worried.

"Yes, I got her voice mail on her cell phone. I didn't leave a message though, because I didn't want to freak her out until I found out what was going on. So what *is* going on? She's my best friend. Is she in any danger?"

Doug exhaled. Adam hadn't been tipped off yet—*maybe*. "Where did they go, Miss White? You said they went away for the weekend. I need to know *where*."

"Sara was all excited about some five star place up in the mountains.

A B&B. Supposed to be real romantic. Oh, God. Who *is* this guy? Is he *dangerous*? *Please*! Tell me what's going on!"

Roy whispered, "I have an address. Midtown, right in my friggin' precinct. I'm calling this in. I want SWAT at his apartment right now."

"He's not going to be there. Just wait a second." He went back to Sharon White. "Do you remember the name of the place? Please, Sharon, this is very important. I need you to really *concentrate*. What was the *name* of the place they were going?"

Sharon tried to think. She was on pain meds from her appendectomy and was a little groggy. "Agent Patmore, honestly, I can't think straight. Adam saved my life. I had an emergency appendectomy. *He* knew I was sick somehow—*I* didn't even know I was sick. He told Sara, and Sara *made* me go to the emergency room. My appendix burst. I might have *died* if he hadn't told Sara. What's going on? Who *is* this guy? How did he *know*?"

"I'm not sure, Sharon. Right now, the main thing is finding your friend. Please. Concentrate. They were going to a bed & Breakfast place…upstate?"

"Yeah, in the mountains." She yawned. "Hold on." Doug could hear a nurse giving her a hard time about being on her phone. She came back, sounding groggier by the second. "I have to go now," she mumbled.

"Put the nurse on the phone, Sharon!" screamed Doug.

He waited through the shuffling of the phone, and a nurse came on rudely. "This patient just had surgery and needs to rest! You will have to call her tomorrow." She hung up.

"Fuck!" screamed Doug. "Let's go!"

"To his apartment?" asked Roy, standing up and grabbing his jacket.

"No! To the hospital to interview Sharon White. The frigging nurse just sedated her in the middle of my goddamned interview! Come on!"

The two of them raced down the hallway towards the garage. "What about his apartment?" screamed Roy, still holding his notes and the printout of Adam's license.

"He's not going to be there! Sharon White says Adam took Sara Somebody up to the mountains to some romantic bed and breakfast place. Adam warned Sharon to get to a hospital right before her appendix burst, so maybe he actually gives a shit about this Sara woman. We need to find them fast. I'll send a team over to his apartment, but you and I need to speak to Sharon!"

Forty-One

New York University Hospital

Doug and Roy made many phone calls between the two of them as they ran to Doug's car. Roy checked with dispatch to find out which hospital Sharon White was in, which took several anxious minutes, while Doug had a tactical team go to Adam's last known address with a forensic team to check the place out. By the time they got to the car, they were both huffing and puffing, excited to finally have a real lead.

They raced across town with lights and sirens and forced their way through the hospital security up to Sharon's room. Sharon's mother was horrified to see the two men bully past the nurses.

"Who are you? My daughter is very sick! She just had surgery! Get out of here!" The nurses were screaming at them as well.

Doug pulled his FBI Badge. "I am Special Agent Doug Patmore. This is a matter of life and death. Sharon's friend Sara is in serious danger and I need to interview Sharon!"

"Well *you* gonna' have to come back *tomorrow*—*this* child is *sleepin!*" barked a large black nurse.

"I am telling you that I am going to speak to this patient, or I will charge you with obstruction of justice! Now wake her up!"

A doctor walked into the room, looking pissed. "Does someone want to tell me what is going on in here? This woman just had surgery! Why are you in here?"

Doug and Roy turned to face the doctor, both of them whipping out their badges.

"NYPD!" snapped Roy. "And this is Agent Patmore, FBI. We need to speak to your patient now or someone may die! Do you understand me? We are trying to save her friend's life!"

Sharon's elderly mother spoke up. "*Whose* life? What's this all about?"

"She has a friend named Sara," said Roy.

"Yes. Sara Lockhart. That's her best friend. She in some kind of danger?" she asked.

"Yes! That's what we are trying to explain. I was interviewing Sharon and a nurse put her to sleep and cut off the phone call!" screamed Doug, his cool demeanor now out the window. "I need to speak to her *right now* or her best friend could be *dead!*"

The doctor spoke quietly. "I will give you a few minutes with her, and then you are to leave her alone and let her get some rest. She just had surgery." He pulled a syringe from his pocket and pushed it into Sharon's IV tube. Sharon's eyes fluttered and she woke up with a yawn, surprised to see so many people in her room.

Forty-Two

Tall Pines

Adam and Sara had walked back to their cottage in uncomfortable silence. Their conversation had gotten dark and worrisome to Sara. She had listened to Adam go on and on about the blood and gore and violence of the war, and it unnerved her. He had been the picture of an ideal boyfriend from the first date until arriving at the lavish Tall Pines resort, but the last conversation was so bizarre, it frightened Sara. She wondered if he had some type of post traumatic stress disorder or something. Was he as "normal" as she had assumed, or was he just another psycho-boyfriend like some of the others she had come across in New York?

They walked back into the cottage, Adam's face looking dark and angry, and Sara's looking upset and gloomy herself. When he closed the door behind them, she burst out.

"I just don't understand how you can bring me up here to the most beautiful place on earth, and then just go off about all those horrible things! I don't know *what* you went through, Adam, but I think it has affected you. I'm not sure I can deal with it if this is how you are. Honestly, Adam, it was a little scary."

Adam was almost ignoring her, taking off his shirt and shoes. She watched him with some alarm, sex being the furthest thing from her mind at that moment.

"Are you listening to me, Adam?"

"Of course I am, Sara. I am sorry to have made you so upset."

Well, at least he apologized, she thought. She still didn't want to kiss and make up quite yet. Adam continued stripping off his clothes as Sara spoke. He pulled the covers of the bed open and slid into it.

"Adam! I am *not* fooling around right now! I'm *serious*. What got into you up there?"

"Just come lay down next to me for a minute," he said in his most charming voice. "I didn't mean to upset you. I have been dealing with a lot of emotions lately that I haven't felt in a very, very, long time." Sara's ice melted just a little.

"What do you mean?" she asked, still standing near the door.

Adam patted the bed next to him. "Come here."

Sara kicked off her shoes and sat next to him, taking off her jacket, but still a bit leery.

"You have made me feel so many things that I am not used to. I didn't realize how lonely I was until I met you, Sara. It was very sudden. Out of nowhere, really."

Sara felt her heart melt and lay down on her side next to him. "I think I know what you mean. I've dated guys over the years, and some were more intense than others, but I've never felt anything like this before, either. It's crazy to think you can love someone that you just met, and I certainly wasn't looking for anything serious. It's not like I was husband shopping or something—but I just, I don't know…"

Adam smiled, his blue eyes shimmering as he gazed at Sara's pretty face, watching the artery in her neck pounding so hard it made the skin move. He could almost *see* the spray.

He patted the bed next to him again. Sara moved closer and gave him a kiss.

"There has never been anyone I thought about sharing forever with, Sara," he said in a soft intense voice. She looked at him and turned to mush. She was in love, just like him.

"Oh, *Adam*," she said, and gave him a hug. He inhaled her smell and felt the heat of her skin. She didn't fight it when he pulled her sweater off, and she slid her jeans off herself. When he reached for her bra, she stopped him.

"Can we just talk a little?" she asked. "I want to lie next to you and feel your body—but I don't want to 'do it' right now, okay?"

"Of course," he said, and pulled her close.

Sara buried her face in his neck and shoulder and hugged him tight. No one had ever discussed "forever" with her before, nor would she have considered it, anyway. But *this* man, that she hardly knew, had somehow made it seem possible. It was overwhelming—sudden and shocking and wonderful.

She said it out loud. "I've never considered anyone as a potential soul mate,' she said softly. "I mean, I've been in love and had boyfriends, but I always knew they weren't *forever*. You make me feel totally different, Adam." She pulled back and smiled. "But you did scare the crap out of me before." Her smile made him smile back. He could smell her chemicals changing. She was warming back up. Fear was changing to feelings of love again. It was closer to the time now.

"Soul mate?" Adam thought to himself. "That would require a soul…"

. . .

ROY AND DOUG WERE ON the roof of the hospital awaiting an FBI helicopter. Doug was on the phone finishing his call as the small black chopper banked its way in. Doug was screaming over the rotors as the chopper touched down. It was a four-seater, with only a pilot in it when it landed.

Doug was in Roy's face yelling over the noise, obviously excited. "It's definitely his apartment! They found a woman's coat in there, and it tested positive for blood and semen. He also had a bunch of women's clothing and all sorts of antiques and weird shit from all over the world. The guy's been collecting trophies for a long time. This is *definitely* our guy!"

Roy and Doug climbed into the back seat of the chopper and said hello to the pilot, who told them to strap in and put on their headphones. The voice activated headphones allowed them to speak to each other inside the small helicopter without yelling.

"I'm Agent Moore. I have your flight plan for Tall Pines Resort up in the Adirondacks. Sit back and enjoy the scenery. It will be a gorgeous ride up. I was told to fly nape of the earth when we get close?"

"Roger that," said Doug. "We are apprehending a possible multiple murder suspect who is extremely dangerous. We won't want to tip him off on the way in. You are to drop us off at the nearest town, about a mile and half away, where the local sheriff will have a car waiting for us.

We'll drive in from there."

"Roger. And I have a standard kit on board below if you need it," said the pilot.

"Excellent. We'll take it when we hit the ground," said Doug.

"What's the kit?" asked Roy.

"Kevlar and automatic weapons. You ever fire a MP-5?"

"Been a while since I handled a machine gun," Roy admitted.

"Just spray and pray," said Doug. "We'll review real fast on the ground." Doug opened his coat and revealed a Marine K-Bar knife. "And I've been saving this for a rainy day,' he said.

"Stake through the heart, huh?" asked Roy.

"Or head on a pike," said Doug.

The two of them spoke to the FBI tactical coordinator at Federal Plaza who was reviewing satellite images of the resort to assist in their apprehension of Adam Priest once they arrived on scene. A second helicopter would be leaving federal Plaza within the hour with a second team of four agents in full tactical gear.

Roy and Doug watched the city of New York disappear behind them as they headed northwest towards their destiny with Adam Priest.

Forty-Three

Tall Pines

Adam had spoken softly and sweetly to Sara, whose guard was now down as she held her lover under the warm covers. They talked about how they met, and how fast it all seemed, but how they both knew this was so different for each of them. They talked about how they could see a long future together. Sara thought it romantic that Adam constantly referred to "forever" with her.

Finally, after much pillow talk, Adam rolled Sara gently on her back and kissed her passionately. He moved to her neck, giving her goose bumps and making her squeal. He allowed his teeth to slide out only a tiny bit—it was so hard to stay under control. As he moved his body against hers, she responded and grinded her hips back against him, moaning softly as he gently sucked her neck.

"Careful," she whispered playfully, "You'll leave a mark!" She giggled and squirmed as he bit a little harder. His needle sharp fangs slid into her skin so gently, she didn't even feel them pierce her neck. He sucked her skin, tasted her blood, and felt his lust rise deep inside him. The animal was trying to get out. It would take every ounce of his being to remain in control as the first few drops of her blood flowed over his tongue. She groaned louder as he sucked her harder, his erection now pressing against her panties, which were getting damp from the inside.

Adam let his stomach empty some of the blood that flowed inside him back up his own throat into the two tiny holes he made in her neck. He only allowed a tiny bit to flow back up into her wound, and then swallowed it all back down. He moved to her mouth and kissed her deeply. Sara was now so turned on she opened her mouth fully, her legs wrapped around Adam as she ground herself against the rod between her legs. She didn't realize what Adam was doing at first, as he exhaled slowly and deeply into her lungs.

At first, she thought it something sexual, allowing him to exhale into her mouth, strange though it was—but he didn't stop. She moved her head away slightly to break the seal on their lips, but Adam held her tight and blew deeper into her lungs.

Sara felt the room spinning. It was going dark. She felt like she was falling, and could hear the noise of thousands of voices screaming out in horror and pain. Adam moved off of her mouth and she tried to push him away—to say something—but nothing would come out of her mouth. Her eyes fluttered, only half open as they rolled back into her head and she stared at infinity. She could hear the sound of her bra ripping, and felt Adam's mouth on her left breast. It seemed like he was biting her so hard, but she couldn't scream. He was tearing off her panties, and her legs just lay spread under him, not fighting, but falling. The room spun faster and she felt dread and horror inside, like she was dying—drowning—disappearing.

Adam entered her with such force that her eyes opened wide for a moment, bringing her back to the present. She looked up at him, and could swear she saw blood on his lips and mouth. She didn't feel pain—didn't feel anything, except his huge erection deep inside her, and it hurt her. He was smiling and seemed to be screaming or howling at her or something, but her world was completely silent. She couldn't hear, couldn't keep him in focus. She was falling falling falling…

Adam was forcing himself into her over and over, biting her breasts and neck, but not tearing her apart. His face had partially changed, showing elongated fang-like teeth, but he had not allowed the monster to fully come out. He held back as hard as he could, howling against the urge to open her throat and drink every last drop. Instead, he refocused his bloodlust sexually, slamming into her as hard as he could, smelling and tasting her different chemicals as she hallucinated.

Sara couldn't speak or scream, as much as she wanted to. She saw images of such terror that her heart was pounding like it was trying to leap through her chest. She could see women torn apart and spraying blood. Adam's face covered in it as he turned into some animal. She saw soldiers with limbs blown off and Adam holding up pieces of what had been humans. The feeling of horror and dread was changing inside her head. It was becoming curiosity. She could feel her real body being pounded up and down as Adam raped her, but she no longer could feel any pain. She looked closer inside her own head at the visions in front of her. She could feel warmth spreading between her legs. She could taste blood in her mouth—and it was not repulsive. It was hot. It was life and energy. Her body felt so hot all over, and every nerve ending was screaming in joy.

The sounds in the room seemed to be slowly returning. She could hear the bed squeaking. Hear Adam grunting and making animal noises. She tried to focus her eyes on him, instead of the endless stream of insane images in her brain. She looked at Adam—saw his face. It wasn't Adam—it was something stronger—something more perfect. She could feel herself orgasm as he also came deep inside her, but in her head, she could see it was a long stream of blood. There was blood everywhere. She was bathing in it as the room started to spin darker again.

The sounds came back, but now they were confusing. She heard an explosion.

· · ·

DOUG AND ROY LANDED IN the middle of a mountain road where a sheriff was waiting with three cars and half a dozen men. He was pissed when Doug and Roy took a car, wearing Kevlar combat vests and carrying small machine guns, and ordered them to stay put. It was *their* county. They didn't like being ordered around by the FBI or some city cop, but they had orders, and they sat and chewed tobacco and spit in anger.

Roy drove like a madman, the car barely hugging the curves of the mountain road. Doug had loaded both weapons and showed Roy how to remove the safety, but advised him to stick with the pistol if the woman was present. The FBI Tactical Team at Federal Plaza had advised the manager of the hotel to stay inside, and keep any guests inside the main building. The manager had given the Feds the cottage number for Adam Priest, and waited for help to arrive.

Roy roared on to the narrow road that led to the make-believe village of small chalets, then slowed down as they looked for chalet number twelve, about halfway down the lane. They hopped out of the car, pulled their weapons, looked at each other, and ran for the door. There was no waiting to get a key. Doug fired a round through the doorknob and Roy kicked the door open as hard as he could. The instant the door flew open, Doug was inside with his Glock 17 up in the two-handed firing position. Roy entered right behind him, weapon drawn and ready like Doug's.

In front of them was a scene from Dante's Inferno. A beautiful young woman was laying spread wide, slick with blood, with some demonic creature from Hell between her legs thrusting away at her. Adam's face was covered in blood, huge fangs out of his mouth, with more blood gurgling up out him with every passing second. He was raping a woman that looked half dead, and he appeared to be in a state of animal rage that was completely unnerving to both officers. They both fired multiple times, screaming in absolute terror as they fired—both of them hit their target over and over.

The thing known as Adam Priest flew off the bed and slammed against the wall, huge chunks of his face and head missing, as nine-millimeter hollow-point rounds impacted through his skull. The creature roared, the sound coming from him nothing from this world. His roar filled the room, and Doug and Roy were still screaming back in stark fear as they continued to fire round after round at the creature. When their clips emptied, they dropped the magazines out of the handles of their Glocks and snapped new ones in the blink of an eye. They approached the creature with weapons extended in front of them. It lay on the floor naked, covered in blood, its back against the wall. It had multiple holes through its face and chest that poured blood out of them, but the thing wasn't dead yet.

Adam eyed the two men and then looked at his own body. He shoved a finger into the hole nearest his heart and pulled it out, looking at the blood in shock. It hurt. He looked up at the two men and spoke, but his voice was a gurgling sound of some Germanic Language they couldn't understand. He was screaming words that meant nothing to them, repeating the phrase "Olmer Bartha" over and over.

Doug stepped closer and emptied his entire clip into the thing's face, until most of his face was unrecognizable pulp. Roy stepped up next to him and emptied his own weapon into the thing's chest where its heart should be. Doug looked at Roy and said, "Fuck this," then knelt down, pulled his K-Bar knife out and grabbing the thing by some hair, cutting and pulling until the thing's head was off. He dropped it on the floor and then shoved his KBar as hard as he could into the thing's chest.

"Stake through the heart," said Roy quietly, still in shock, his hands shaking as he fought the urge to vomit.

"Stake through the heart," repeated Doug, also shaken to the edge of sanity. The head was next to the body, huge fangs extending from the mouth, as the silvery eyes went black and dead.

Roy looked at the woman on the bed and ran over to her. "Not much of a pulse. Looks like he was almost done with her." Roy pulled his radio and called for paramedics to Tall Pines immediately.

Doug grabbed blankets and started wrapping the girl. "Quick! Help me wrap her up and get her out of here. We're going to torch this fucking thing. "I'm not taking any chances!"

Roy and Doug wrapped the woman tightly with sheets and blankets, her face white with blue lips. Her eyes were almost closed completely. They rushed her out of the chalet and laid her in the backseat of their car, then ran back inside the room. There was a large stone fireplace that had starter logs near a pile of real wood. Doug began working and

Roy just followed his lead. They took what had been Adam Priest and shoved him against the corner of the room, covered him with starter logs and real wood, shoved newspaper and magazines all over him, and lit the logs.

The starter logs lit immediately, catching the paper and filling the room with light blue smoke. Doug reloaded his Glock, fired another seventeen rounds into whatever was left of the thing's head until it broke into small pieces, and the two of them watched the room start to catch fire. When the fire reached the drapes and the smoke thickened around the burning corpse, the two of them backed out of the room. They ran back to the car and Doug pulled his radio.

"Team Two! This is Agent Patmore. Subject is down. I repeat— subject is down. We have a female in need of immediate medical assistance. She is not conscious and has lost a lot of blood. She has a very weak pulse, but we are going to lose her if we can't get her to a hospital immediately. Bring the chopper directly here and get her aboard. She's needs to be Medivaced immediately."

"I called for an ambulance," said Roy quietly, watching the sheets turning red with blood.

"She'll never make it by car. Hell—she won't make it by chopper. Jesus fucking Christ, Roy. You see that thing's fucking face?" It was a rhetorical question. Doug was in shock as much as Roy was.

They could hear rotor blades thumping over the tree tops, and the chopper banked hard when the pilot saw them standing in the parking lot. A few curious vacationers peered through stain glass windows as they watched a chalet begin to burn behind two men dressed for combat.

The chopper landed, and two Feds in black combat gear jumped from the rear seat. They helped Roy and Doug load the woman into the rear seat and belt her down as best they could, then slam the door and watch as the pilot took off to the nearest hospital.

The two feds noticed the flames coming out of the building. "You call that in yet?" one of them asked.

"Nope," said Doug quietly. "Let it burn."

Forty-Four

Greater Albany General Hospital

Doug and Roy drove with the two agents that had given up their seats to the nearest hospital, which happened to be east of where they were and not exactly on the way home. It was over an hour away at the speed they were driving, with lights flashing all the way. They were almost there when the call came in over the radio.

Doug picked it up immediately. He and Roy were in the back seat, exhausted. "This is Patmore, go ahead," he said.

"Agent Patmore, this is Agent Colgan. I flew in with the girl and the pilot. I tried my best to stop the bleeding on the way in, and even tried CPR en route. We had a crash cart and docs waiting for her when we got here, but it was no use. They worked on her for thirty minutes and gave her five units of blood while they were working on her, but I'm sorry to tell you, she didn't make it."

Doug's head fell back against the seat. He looked at Roy. "She didn't make it."

"Fuck," said Roy quietly.

"You want us to keep going? We're almost there," said the driver.

"Yeah. We'll take the chopper back from the hospital and the sheriff can pick up his car there whenever. Anyway, I want to see the body."

Roy looked at him. "Ain't we seen enough?" he asked. They both looked like they had been through a war.

"Closure. I don't know. I want to see her."

They drove in silence the rest of the way and pulled up front where two agents were standing awaiting their arrival.

"Sorry, Doug. You guys did a great job. You got that sick fuck. At least it's over. This way."

The group walked quietly to the elevator and took the trip down to the morgue. A Medical Examiner was waiting for them.

"Gentlemen. She's over here. There's nothing you could have done. She had lost so much blood. Looks like she got attacked by a bear or something." They walked through a set of doors to a gurney that was drenched in blood, a green sheet on the floor. There was no body on the gurney.

The doc's face fell. "She was right there a second ago. Who the hell moved her? There's no one else down here?…"